NEVER OUT OF MIND

K. MCCRAE

K. MCCRAE BOOKS

Copyright © K.McCrae, 2022

All rights reserved

First published 2022

The moral right of the author has been asserted

ISBN: 978-1-8380322-3-4 (Paperback)
ISBN: 978-1-8380322-2-7 (eBook)

All characters and events in this publication are fictitious, and any resemblance to actual persons, living or dead, is purely coincidental.

1

Eleanor stood in the kitchen doorway, her hands trembling. Strands of dark hair had fallen loose from her ponytail and now clung to her skin with sweat.

'There is a body in the garden.' Her voice was calm and pragmatic. Her mind still numb from the shock.

'Those damn foxes,' Darryl said. His face half-hidden inside a large cardboard box on the kitchen counter. Stained from damp and dust after years buried in his loft. He lifted out an item wrapped in an old, yellowed newspaper and unravelled it.

It was no surprise that his first thought went to foxes. It had become a regular occurrence to find mauled and half-eaten poultry in their garden.

'The farmer's not going to have any chickens left at this rate,' Darryl continued, carefully revealing a stone lump of something or other. One of his archaeological finds from over the years. He wrapped it again and put it back in the box. 'Don't worry, I'll come and get rid of it. I'm almost done here.'

'No, not a chicken. A body. There is a dead body in the garden. Under the patio. A dead, human body.' The trembling had now reached Eleanor's voice. Red, raw nail marks stung where she had been scratching anxiously at the dried mud on her hands.

'You're kidding.' Darryl pulled his head out of the box and looked at her, an excited glaze over his eyes.

Eleanor could only shake her head. The muscles in her jaw would no longer let her form words. A huge grin appeared on Darryl's face.

'That's amazing. I can't believe it. I wonder if it's related to the Minstrel-wood site.'

Eleanor exhaled hard. *Of course,* she thought, *Heaven forbid it could be anything other than an ancient site just waiting for him to reveal its secrets.* Sometimes she wished he could remove his archaeologist hat and remain in the present world for a while.

'Darryl,' she forced out, but it was only a whisper.

'Another mausoleum? No, it can't be.' Darryl's eyes darted round the room as though searching his thoughts. 'We're too far out—'

'Darryl,' she implored, fighting for his attention.

'But if it is, this could change—'

'Darryl,' Eleanor finally shouted. She appreciated he enjoyed his new job, but now was not the time for his enthusiasm.

'But this is fantastic,' he interrupted. 'We've only found two mausolea, a third would be incredible. And this far out from the site. Or it could be remains from a completely different, or maybe an earlier site. I've got to have a look.' Darryl gave a small skip as he ran past her and out the back door.

Eleanor, dumbfounded, stared after him in silence. There was no use following him. He'd be back soon, anyway. She had often found his easygoing manner a calming antidote during her more distressing moments of grief. But there were times, like now, when it was just plain insensitive.

She took these few quiet moments to calm her breathing.

Pacing the room, she waited for Darryl's return. Hunching her shoulders, she popped a jacket over them in an attempt to take the chill from her bones. The small windows inset into the thick walls were determined to keep out the warmth. A coldness filled the room on the hottest of days. Though now she needed more than a jacket to warm her.

Pulling up the patio slabs had seemed a good excuse as an escape from the cold, claustrophobic house and into the light of the sun. Left unchecked for the last twenty years, the roots of an old cherry tree had created an expanse of uneven and broken flagstones as nature endeavoured to break free from its binds. A job that needed doing, but of no real urgency compared to inside the house. But now, the job had brought about a more pressing concern.

Her deep breaths juddered as she waited in the silence. It was a futile attempt to exhale the shock of what she had discovered and to push memories of deaths closer to home out of her mind. Darryl returned and his silhouette stood in the doorway, the sun lowering just below the top of the door frame.

'That's no Roman,' he said, subdued.

'No,' Eleanor said. Calmer now and more able to think.

'It's been there a while, by the looks of it, but certainly not 1600 years or so.'

'No,' she repeated.

Darryl stepped further into the room. The sun shone through the open doorway and lit his pale face.

'I'm so sorry. I'm so, so sorry.' He marched over to Eleanor and engulfed her in his arms.

The safety of his grasp finally released Eleanor's tears.

∼

Darryl called the police while Eleanor poured herself a scotch. Then they waited, huddled together on the sofa. Neither knowing what to say and lost in their own thoughts.

As an archaeologist, Darryl had dealt with skeletons before. An air of excitement would surround the site whenever somebody discovered a burial. But this was different. Examining a grave that had originated hundreds of years previously required a certain detachment. Their life, their living, breathing time on this planet was a mystery to uncover. Simply part of the job. Landing on his knees in the dirt, eager to unearth another puzzle, the shock had almost choked him. To see a skeleton in modern clothing, even just a small section as he had seen here, was something he could not detach himself from. The once brightly coloured clothes, now barely rags, clung to the bones after years of the earth's weight pressing down on them. He was left with a turbulent sensation under his skin and a foul taste in his mouth.

'They're here,' he said, though his announcement wasn't necessary. The sun had disappeared and the police car's headlights shone brightly through the window as they pulled up. They made their way to the front door together and Darryl opened it, trying his best at a cordial greeting. Everything from then on was a blur. Strangers took over. Statements were given. And now, Eleanor sat at the kitchen table while Darryl paced the room, clenching his hands in agitation. Glancing at Eleanor, he saw her hand tremble as she reached for her glass of scotch. A hard line at her wrists created by her gardening gloves, which had hidden her hands from the sun while her forearms burned with sunburn. She took a moment to steady herself before lifting the glass. Darryl joined her as she returned her glass to the table, jumping at the loud bang as she misjudged the placement, and it hit a little too hard.

He held her hands and berated himself again for not

seeing her distress earlier, especially after what she had been through. The loss of both her husband and son over a year ago still haunted her. He had been so caught up on uncovering his finds that he had packed away years ago, when Eleanor mentioned a human body, he naturally assumed it was a Roman. After all, the large Roman site where he worked wasn't far. Surely she would understand. He squeezed her hands gently out of guilt. Who was he kidding? He squeezed tighter still at the thought of the reality of what was in their garden.

Darryl had lost all track of time and so had no idea how long it was before the man who had initially introduced himself as DCI Hanson returned to the kitchen from the garden. Eleanor now had a little colour in her face and jumped up when he entered.

'Would you like a tea or coffee?' She headed for the kettle.

'Only if you're certain, but that would be nice. Tea, please.' The DCI joined Darryl at the table. 'I have some questions for you both if that's OK?' Neither Darryl nor Eleanor voiced an objection and so DCI Hanson continued. 'How long have you lived here?'

'We moved in just over three weeks ago. We plan on renovating the entire building and — I'm sorry, you don't need to know that.' Darryl looked away in his embarrassment. Nerves were getting the better of him.

'That's OK,' the DCI said. 'It'll be nice to see the old place looked after again.'

His voice was gentle and friendly, his demeanour relaxed. Although in a suit, his tie was pulled slightly loose at the neck, easing his air of authority. Darryl wondered if they had special training for these circumstances. *How to put a member of public at ease if they find a body in their garden. What a stupid thing to think.* Darryl forced himself to focus.

'Were you living nearby before you moved here?' The DCI asked.

'No, we moved up from near Chartford Brooke, about four hours' drive south of here.'

'How much do you know about the history of this place?' DCI Hanson asked.

'I believe it's early seventeenth century, but I need to do some more research to narrow down the date further.' Darryl stopped at the look from Eleanor.

'I meant more recent history,' The DCI said with a slight smile.

'Nothing really. I know it's been empty for the last twenty years, but why, I don't know. It was like the Mary Celeste when we moved in.' Darryl gave a nervous laugh.

'I'm sorry, Mary...' the DCI looked puzzled.

'Mary Celeste. The ship that was discovered drifting in the latter half of the 1800s with no crew on board.' The DCI's puzzled expression hadn't changed, so Darryl continued. 'Their possessions were still in place... It's a very famous mystery. Obviously, with the use of modern scientific resources, there are theories as to what happened, but I don't think we'll ever know for certain.' Darryl's brain suddenly saw a connection. 'Is that who's in the garden? Whoever lived here?'

The shock forced him to stand, pushing his chair out behind him. A crash came from behind as Eleanor dropped a mug.

'How many people lived here? Are there more of them out there?'

'At this stage, we don't know who it is, but there is no need for you to concern yourself. We will be doing a thorough investigation of the entire area. Depending on circumstances, we may need to ask you to vacate the house. That may not be necessary,' DCI Hanson quickly added at the gasps that came from both Darryl and Eleanor, 'but I wanted to give you some prior warning. Thank you,' he said with a soft smile as Eleanor placed a mug of hot tea on the table in front of him, his large dark eyes peering from under his dark fringe.

'Now, Mrs Garrett, I understand it was you that originally made the discovery?'

'Yes,' she whispered.

'Can I ask why you started digging in that one particular place?'

'The roots,' she stuttered. 'The tree roots. They were pushing up the patio slabs. I - I just wanted to clear them. Clear them out of the way. There is so much that needs doing, it just - it just seemed like a good place to start.'

'I see, and Mr Westwood, you were still in the house?'

'Yes, I stayed inside. As Eleanor said, there is a lot to do both inside and out.'

'OK,' DCI Hanson stood, stretching his long legs that had been cramped under the table. 'That will be all from me for now. I hope you enjoy your time at the house and it's good to see the ghost stories haven't turned you off,' he said with an easy going laugh.

Aware that his laughter was louder than usual, Darryl was trying too hard to keep his panic under control. He had never mentioned the stories he had heard to Eleanor, and this probably would not have been the best time for her to hear about them.

Eleanor simply stared at him.

'Nothing, really.' He wrinkled his nose in contempt at the idea.

'I'll leave you my card,' DCI Hanson said. He reached into his inside jacket pocket and pulled out a card. Leaving it on the table, he headed for the back door. 'I'm sure we'll see each other again, it's a small village. Mrs Garrett, Mr Westwood.' He nodded and left into the sound of people still busy in the garden.

'Ghosts?' Eleanor asked.

'It was nothing, honestly. Just some silly kids' stories about wailing and noises coming from the house when it was empty. Usual kids' stuff.'

'Maybe that's why the place was left unoccupied for twenty years,' she said.

'Absolutely,' Darryl said sarcastically. 'It was nothing to do with the rot, the cracks, the rat infestation.' He paused and cradled Eleanor's hands. 'Look, have you heard any wailing? Have you heard any unexplained noises?'

So certain that she couldn't say yes to either of these questions, he continued.

'Kids like to make up stories about spooky-looking houses. But you and I know that it's not spooky. It's just sad, even pitiful. But we're going to change all that. We're going to be happy here, make memories here. Bring it back to life. Aren't we?'

Eleanor's nod was given begrudgingly. Even so, he was grateful it was a nod. He held her in his arms, her body rigid. He had been so excited about finding this house; it had been a lifelong dream to renovate such a property that he hadn't thought about the toll it may take for someone who didn't have the same attachment for its history, its uniqueness.

'It'll be beautiful, I promise you. And it will be worth it.'

～

That evening, Eleanor sat in the bath, hugging her knees tightly. The water was cold against her skin. She dipped her head forward and her long brown hair fell round her face like a veil, shutting out the immediate surroundings. The cracked tiles, a cupboard door hanging off its hinges, and paint peeling from the ceiling. Only the internal issues concerned her now.

An hour had passed. She had scrubbed away the mud and sweat from her work in the garden. The sight of the bones couldn't be so easily washed away. The vision replayed itself again and again in her mind. Appearing through the earth as though digging for potatoes; ascending through the broken soil as her fork had loosened the years of dense, compact earth. Leaving her with an inexplicable sense of violation.

Now, in her bath, surrounded by chaos, she also found her sanctuary. Time and space to let the events of the day sink in. A luxury she could not have while Darryl was trying too hard to accommodate her. Constantly at her side, as though she may break at any moment.

She had often questioned her judgement, or even her sanity, as to why she had agreed to buy such a catastrophe of a house with Darryl. There seemed no time to breathe before the next problem arose from the dust and soot. Some problems were only to be expected in a house left to deteriorate for twenty years. But then there were the issues that came with a house of this age. It had picked up a few problems over its four hundred years. Darryl had convinced her of the dream home it would become. He had filled her head with the idyllic country cottage, complete with the stereo-typical roses round the doorway. His enthusiasm had blinded her. Now, living amongst it all for the past three weeks, she was having trouble seeing that vision. Unable to see past certain other issues. The ten-foot crack in the side wall was more than a little worrying. Rot in the wooden window frames, some to the extent where it seemed impossible for the glass to remain in place. Sloping floors upstairs. Not only loose and creaky floorboards downstairs, but extensive areas where there were no floorboards at all, just bare earth. They had done their best to cover it with large sheets of plywood balanced on the floor joists, but their make-shift solution wobbled noisily with every step. And now, a body in the garden.

She had thought she'd be safe outside. What could go wrong in the garden? Patio slabs unseated by a few sprawling tree roots. A morning with the brambles, scratching their revenge at being uprooted. Brambles she could cope with, but a dead body? The discovery had been a shock, there was no doubting that, but the body was from years ago. There was no personal connection, and the police would handle it from here. It was no more than an inconvenience that they couldn't use their garden while the police investigated. Or so she tried to tell herself.

The one thing she couldn't get off her mind was the ghost stories. She didn't care about the stories themselves; she never had concerned herself with these things. Like Darryl had said, it would have been kids making up stories. She had done the same as a child. The actual issue was Darryl hadn't told her. She understood his concern for her during her frequently broken nights. Nightmares involving her husband and son, Nick and Chris, and the torment of their deaths were a regular occurrence, but there was nothing he could do or say that would help. Did he think her so fragile that she wouldn't be able to cope with a couple of kids' stories, though in reality she had to endure much more real and physical problems? A couple of spectral spirits may have been a welcome change to the persistent rats she kept finding round the house. Maybe he hadn't wanted to run the risk of her not wanting the house in the first place? Or was he simply just susceptible to keeping secrets? The answer to that question scared her more than any ghost could, no matter how many times she told herself to stop being so melodramatic.

2

Darryl pushed his old thin cotton jumper into his leather satchel.

'I'm sorry to be leaving you with all this. Are you sure you'll be OK?' His gaze followed the kitchen counter-tops, searching for his phone.

He was still too early to leave for work, but it was clear he was keen to get out of the house. A feeling Eleanor could understand.

'I'll be fine.' She tried to sound convincing, but she knew he could see through it. In truth, she didn't know what she was going to do. The police had cordoned off most of the garden, leaving only the footpath that led to the driveway. Although she would have avoided it anyway, but then she wanted to avoid the house too. Another day in the cold and gloom. A depressing thought.

'Why don't I drive you into the village? You can have a wander and walk back later. Get some fresh air away from the house. Or just keep walking if things are that bad,' Darryl added with a nervous laugh.

She ignored his last remark. A fleeting resentment chilled

her. Darryl had the luxury of working five days a week, away from the stress of the house. While she, with no job to go to, felt permanently suffocated. Positives were sparse and became fewer with each day that passed. Getting out for a walk gave a glimpse of optimism. Some time to regain a bit of perspective. Just the thought relaxed her, and she breathed more easily.

'We need a few bits. You can drop me at the village shop.' She surprised herself with the excitement in her voice. 'Have you got time to wait while I get ready? Won't be a tick.'

∽

Ten minutes later, they climbed into Darryl's old Land Rover and were making their way noisily along the narrow country roads towards Bramblemere.

'If we're stopping at the shop, we could do some investigating of our own?' Darryl said. 'We were quite good at it before.'

'We were both nearly killed,' Eleanor replied incredulously.

'Maybe so,' he shrugged. 'But we still got our man.'

'More by luck than judgement.' Eleanor had tried to block out the memory of the last time they had come face to face with a killer. 'No,' she said, quietly, but firmly.

'Come on, I've still got some time,' Darryl persisted. 'We can ask a few questions about who they were and if they had any enemies. Someone from round here may remember them. The house isn't that far out of the village and in a place this size everybody knows everybody else, as well as what they're up to.'

'I just want a quiet walk,' Eleanor interrupted, irritated by Darryl's enthusiasm. She wanted to forget ever seeing the body. In her head she could still hear the dull knock of the bones as she dug the earth beneath the slabs and they fell against her fork. She didn't want to be reminded of the overwhelming sickness as she realised what she had discovered. 'I don't want to investigate,' she went on. 'We don't know what we'd find.'

'It was years ago. Whoever did it is probably long gone if that's worrying you. Nobody's going to hang around waiting for a dead body to be dug up. They would have left pretty damn quick unless they're stupid. We won't be in any danger. Don't you want to know who they were, what they did—'

'No. No, I don't,' Eleanor snapped. 'They're not one of your damn Romans just lying there waiting for you to come along and analyse. Let the police deal with it. As far as I'm concerned, they're nothing but an intruder on our property.'

'I'm sorry,' Darryl said after a moment's silence. The energy gone from his voice. 'You're right. For work, I've learnt to think of them as evidence of a time in history. I guess I was trying to do the same here. To be honest, after yesterday, I don't think I'll ever look at one of my damn Romans in quite the same way again.'

'You investigate. It's what you do,' Eleanor said apologetically, realising he had been just as affected by the body's discovery as she had. What she had taken for enthusiasm was more likely to be nervous tension. 'And you're right, they deserve more than being hidden in a stagnant hole. But now we've found them, the police can contact their family and send them home. We've done our part.'

'OK, no investigating, I promise.' Darryl pulled up outside the village shop and switched off the engine. 'Still, our first visit here, we should make a bit of an effort to introduce ourselves and make sure they have a good supply of bread and milk.'

'I was thinking more of cake.'

'And cake,' Darryl repeated with a laugh.

~

Darryl opened the door of the village shop and the dingle of a small bell above his head greeted him. A warm orange glow came from the single light bulb in the centre of the ceiling. The bright morning sunlight hadn't yet made it through the oversized shop window. The building, though looking out over the sunlit village green, was still in shadow. A strong contrast to the brightly lit shops in Northwood Gate town centre and the welcome muted light gave a homely atmosphere. The small shop afforded other benefits, too. No need to jostle with the many tourists that swamped the town, for one. And, after several encounters with rude shop assistants, no doubt there would be a friendlier service. Shelving units created three aisles where a lounge would have been in the converted house, and Darryl took the central one. He explored the range of produce, which gradually got darker the lower they went as they descended further out of the light's reach. But they had everything he could imagine he would need living in a village without wanting to take the extra half-hour trip into town. The top of Eleanor's head glided along in the next aisle until she stopped. He guessed she'd found the cake section.

Directly ahead, a woman walked into view and stood behind a small counter. Behind her, and to one side, was an open doorway, presumably leading to the living area. She greeted them with a bright, cheerful face. Her fair hair pulled back in a crude bun with more than a few strands escaping the clasp, though she had a confidence that said she didn't care.

'Good morning,' she said cheerily. 'Can I help you?'

The opening of the shop door interrupted Darryl's attempt to introduce himself. A woman's voice smothered the sound of the bell with excited chatter as soon as the door opened.

'Well, you'll never guess what's happened. Miss Starling has turned up buried in her own gar—' She stopped mid-flow, her mouth open wide, her eyes almost as wide as her mouth.

The woman, who had been hidden behind various food and household items, had taken the quickest route to pass on her gossip until she'd suddenly appeared at the opposite end of the aisle. Darryl had followed the sound of her voice until he was confronted by a small woman with a head of tight blond curls and thick make-up.

'Good morning, I'm Stella,' she said, ignoring her friend, who had given an audible gasp at her news. Stella hitched her bag further onto her shoulder and pushed her shoulders back as though trying to make herself taller.

'Darryl and Eleanor—' Stella's curiosity cut Darryl's introduction short.

'You're the new owners of Rushmere cottage, aren't you?' Her pride at knowing this information exuded from her. She somehow had a way of looking down her nose at Darryl and Eleanor, even though she was at least ten inches shorter than him.

Darryl nodded and was about to express their intentions for the renovation when Stella continued.

'I thought so. We're a tiny village here and not much happens. So, when somebody moves in to the local haunted house, it's big news.'

'Big news? Not as big as Miss Starling, was that the name?' Darryl said wryly.

He had taken an immediate dislike to Stella with her pompous voice and conceited attitude.

'Yes, Miss Starling,' she said with a snide smile, hesitating, as though deciding whether she should say anymore. 'We had all believed she'd run off into the sunset with her boyfriend. Next thing we know, it looks like she's turned up buried in her garden - your garden.' A sudden flailing of her arms caused her bag to slip from her shoulder down into the crook of her elbow.

'You both knew her?' Darryl asked, instantly regretting he had. He could sense Eleanor's eyes boring into him.

'I would just like to clarify that it has not yet been confirmed that it is Miss Starling. Carl would never forgive me if I said it was. But, in my mind, they don't need to confirm it. They even found her suitcase buried along with her.'

Darryl briefly wondered who Carl was. A quick glance towards the woman behind the counter in hope of some help showed she hadn't moved since her initial shock at Stella's announcement. Her face was pale, and she gazed into the air, seemingly unaware of the conversation in front of her.

'But, of course, we all heard what happened when she went missing. Do you remember, Al?' Stella hitched her bag onto her shoulder again as she flicked a glance towards the woman behind the counter.

A nod came in answer, jolting the woman back into the present. A little colour returning to her cheeks.

'Becky, one of the teachers at the school in the village here, used to work with her. She was Miss Starling's TA back then. That stands for Teaching Assistant,' she added patronisingly. 'She told us all about how Miss Starling would go on and on about her boyfriend who was going to come and join her, didn't she, Al?' She flicked another glance in the general direction of her friend. 'I don't think I ever even knew her first name. She was always just Miss Starling to us. To be honest, we all thought she was a bit strange, always kept herself to herself.' She took a large breath before beginning again.

'Anyway, none of us ever imagined that she could be buried in her own garden.' She suddenly turned to Eleanor with a furrowed brow. 'Carl told me how shook up you were yesterday. I hope you're feeling a bit better today.'

She took hold of Eleanor's hands, false sympathy pouring

from her eyes. Something about Eleanor's hands caught Stella's attention.

'Oh, you are married.' Her well-manicured hands ran over Eleanor's ring. 'But Carl gave different names for you both.' She glanced at Darryl's left hand, where there was no ring. Her well-plucked eyebrows raised with curiosity, and an internal sneer revealed itself slightly in the corner of her mouth. 'I — I'm sorry, it's none of my business.' She dropped Eleanor's hand with a slight laugh and paused, as though hoping one of them would explain.

Darryl could have explained how Eleanor's family had been killed in a car crash, but it wasn't his story to tell. Instead, he put his arm around Eleanor's shoulders and pulled her in. He would not let some busy body try to make them feel inferior.

'Who's Carl?' he said bluntly, taking advantage of the pause and trying not to let the animosity sound in his voice.

'Oh, sorry. My mouth just runs away with me sometimes. I just assume everyone knows my husband, Carl, being such an important person in the community. He's the Detective Chief Inspector that spoke to you yesterday.' She enunciated each word of his title with pride. 'In fact, it was this case that made Carl decide to join the police force all those years ago. He always knew they had it wrong. Oh, and I nearly forgot,' she said, flailing her arms in a panic and turning to her friend again. Her tight curls bouncing with the movement. 'I was just talking to Becky when dropping off Tommy - that's my sister's boy,' she said with a quick flick of her head towards Darryl and Eleanor. 'She told me that Isabelle was taken in to hospital last night - that's her assistant,' another quick flick. 'She's gone into labour and she's only twenty-four weeks gone. It's far too early. How devastating it would be for her to lose her child.'

Darryl felt Eleanor's body stiffen. His glimpse towards her showed she held a large loaf of crusty bread. Nail indentations along the sides. Talk of losing a child would not help her already fragile state. He squeezed her shoulders and willed her to know that he was there for her. An early exit to the shop was called for without wanting to be rude; it was their first time in there, after all. But Stella didn't stop and continued her narrative.

Turning her attention back to Darryl and Eleanor, she said, 'I don't have children of my own, but I do have a very strong maternal instinct.' She leaned closer and added in a loud whisper, 'Unfortunately, Carl can't have children.'

At this point, Darryl choked on his sudden intake of air. Friendly banter is all very well, but where did this woman draw the line? The Detective Chief Inspector they had met yesterday was nothing but caring and diplomatic. The opposite of his wife.

'Anyway, now Becky's having terrible trouble trying to find someone to cover for Isabelle. Her maternity leave cover can't start for another four weeks.' Stella's head bobbed from one person to another, making certain everybody heard the latest gossip, before settling on her old friend. 'I'll have a latte this morning, if you wouldn't mind, Al.'

The woman behind the counter turned stiffly to a large, modern coffee machine that looked incongruous in the homely shop. Darryl noticed her clenching her fists, her knuckles white.

'Anyway, must run. Just needed to grab my morning coffee. Don't want to risk winding down in the middle of the morning,' continued Stella, steam hissing loudly behind the counter. 'I have a client coming to see old Fred's place in town. He was killed in a car accident just along from you, in fact, a few months ago. Black spot bridge we call it, I won't bore you with the details, but it was a terrible loss. Amazing apartment, though. I'd have it myself if I could. But not everyone likes all the mod cons. They want something with character these days. Personally, I think it has quite enough character of its own.'

A large paper cup with steam rising out of a small hole in the lid appeared on the counter-top.

'There I go blabbering on again. I'm going to get myself into so much trouble one of these days with this mouth of mine.' Stella handed over her card and took a sip of her steaming latte as though ingesting a shot of heroin. After she retrieved her card, she left as quickly as she had appeared. The shop itself seemed to sigh with relief in the quiet that followed.

'And I thought I had too much caffeine,' Eleanor said, finally.

'Is that... normal?' Darryl struggled to find a word to describe Stella that wouldn't be rude.

'That's Stella,' the woman behind the counter exhaled a long breath and leisurely leaned on the counter. 'Stuck-up Stella, she's known as in the village. I won't insult your intelligence by explaining why.'

'She's really quite something,' Darryl said. 'I don't think I can remember half the things she said.'

'Not surprising. Bullet points are available for a small fee.'

Her sarcasm appealed to Darryl's sense of humour.

'The trick is to just keep quiet till she's finished and gone. I'm Alison, by the way, but she does insist on calling me Al. I can cope with Ali, but Al?' She pulled a face.

'I'm guessing she's an estate agent,' Darryl said, sensing that Eleanor didn't want to join in the conversation.

'Yes,' Alison drawled. 'My theory is that she intimidates her clients into submission, as she did with me.' She pulled another face and glanced over at the shiny silver coffee machine. 'That bloody coffee. I don't know why she doesn't just go into one of the coffee shops in town where her office is. Heaven knows there are enough of them. But no. Somehow, she persuaded me to install one of these new machines. It took me a week to work out how to use it. Apparently, it's for my own benefit. When the tourists come out this far, I'll be grateful I can serve them proper coffee. "Have to keep up with the new," she says. Well, I'm still waiting for those tourists.'

Darryl had the feeling that Alison wasn't as fond of Stella as Stella was of Alison, but he also got the impression that people here didn't get the chance to talk much. He surreptitiously glanced at his watch as she continued.

'Becky, the teacher, is the only one who has any patience with her. She will actually attempt a conversation instead of just waiting for her to stop and leave like the rest of us do. I guess she gets a lot of practice working with small children. It's more than I could ever do. The patience of a saint, that woman.' Alison finished with an enormous sigh. 'And that's about it. Now you know all there is to know about us. Welcome to Bramblemere.'

Darryl laughed at her sarcasm and was about to make their apologies for leaving when another voice interrupted.

'Not quite all of us.' A man wearing a postman's uniform walked through the doorway from the living accommodation.

Darryl recognised him. He had often seen him delivering to Rushmere cottage. He took another anxious look at his watch, even though only a minute had passed.

'My husband,' Alison said. Her eyes lowered as she spoke, as though admitting something awful, and her previous confidant demeanour took a step back.

'Shaun,' the man said, reaching out to shake Darryl's hand.

'Darryl, and Eleanor.'

Shaun swung open the counter-top and moved further into the shop. 'Eleanor, what a beautiful name.' He didn't shake Eleanor's proffered hand, instead he kissed it, watching her intently. 'Somebody caught the sun,' he said, gently running his fingers along Eleanor's bright red forearm.

She pulled her arm away forcefully, and Shaun laughed. Eleanor had mentioned her dislike for the postman, who seemed to hang around too long, but he had thought her paranoid. Just something else to complain about. Maybe she hadn't been so paranoid after all.

'Shaun, leave it. You never know where these things lead.' Alison said with a playful tone to her voice, but her smile was false and she avoided looking directly at him.

'You're from Rushmere Cottage, aren't you?' he said, directing his question towards Eleanor.

'Yes,' she replied quietly.

'Maybe I'll come knocking on your door sometime,' he said. 'I may have the odd parcel to deliver now and again.'

'I've seen you hanging about outside the house.' Her intonation changed at Shaun's insinuation.

Her voice was strong, and her stress on the words *hanging about* made Darryl wonder whether she had felt threatened by him and he fought the urge to step in and protect her.

'Just doing my job,' Shaun continued, 'but I'll take it as a compliment that you've noticed me. When required, I can take on extra little jobs,' he whispered.

Alison coughed loudly, and Shaun returned to his wife's side. Putting his arm around her shoulders, he continued, 'Trips to Northwood Gate if you ever need something picked up, dry cleaning and such likes,' he clarified.

Alison didn't look impressed. Her shoulders had stiffened at his touch. 'Are you staying long?' she asked.

Darryl's liking for this woman suddenly changed. 'Yes,' he answered. 'We hope to do the old place up and live there for *many* years.'

3

Eleanor left the shop and breathed in the fresh springtime air, filling her lungs with freedom in an attempt to stop the churning in her stomach. The sun was still low, its warmth not yet in full force. The air cool and bracing. There was no doubting the reason for Stuck-up Stella's nickname. Distracting herself with the discovery of the delicious-looking, though limited selection, of home-made cakes, was partially successful. The small, freshly baked bakery section was a welcome sight after the disappointing first display she had found in the aisle. Paltry and uninspiring were the words that came to mind. But her diversionary tactic was short-lived.

Stella's less than diplomatic glances towards her ring began the downward spiral and things got worse from there. Each mention of children, the school, the ordeal of losing a child, reverberated through her body and twisted the knot in her throat tighter until she could hardly breathe. Outwardly she tried to smile through the pain, inwardly she was crumbling. From his blunt tone, Darryl had obviously taken a dislike to her, too, and had tried to support Eleanor emotionally while she herself, out of sheer desperation, had picked up a crusty loaf and dug her nails into the sides.

Finally, the ordeal was over, or so she had thought. Shaun was quite something else. Eleanor's skin crawled at his quiet, husky voice. A natural attribute, or was it intentional? An excuse to move closer or a quality he thought women desired? Either way, it repulsed her, and she recoiled at his touch.

Relieved to get out of the shop, she could breathe again, the air drying her eyes.

Darryl placed their shopping in the car and gave Eleanor a peck goodbye.

'Are you sure you're going to be alright?' he asked, now hurrying to get to work on time.

Eleanor nodded. She stared unseeing at the village green. Darryl gently took hold of her hands, jolting her back to reality. She hadn't realised until then she had been playing with her ring again.

'We know why you're wearing it and that's all that matters,' he said. 'It's none of their business.'

A small, nervous laugh erupted from Eleanor. 'Do you mind? Mind me wearing it, I mean?'

'No. No, I don't. I know what it means to you. You keep it on as long as you like.'

She relaxed a little before Darryl broke the quiet moment between them.

'I've got to go or I'm going to be late.' He rushed to climb in to the other side of the car. 'See you later. Call me at lunchtime.'

'Maybe,' she called back. 'If I feel like it,' she replied, mimicking nonchalance.

He drove off at speed, leaving Eleanor standing at the side of the road. Unsure whether she felt relieved or abandoned. She closed her eyes, wanting to shut out the world. Once the rattles of the Land

Rover had left earshot, there was silence in every direction. Only birdsong interrupted the quiet. As she listened, she noticed more and more intermittent chirping. The darkness of her eyelids turned a warm red and Eleanor could feel she was no longer in shadow. She consciously took a deep breath and pulled her shoulders down. She opened her eyes and took in the beauty of her surroundings, willing an end to her current situation. Hoping for a time when she could enjoy conversations without the feeling of constant dread.

The village green, directly opposite, was framed by the olde worlde buildings Darryl was so fond of. A small, stubby church peeped out above a row of terraced cottages to her left, and to her right was a primary school that had the appearance of a miniature manor house. A large entrance door and grandiose windows, but for little people. To the far side of the green was the obligatory village pub, *The Cat and Kitten,* completing the country idyll.

Eleanor began the slow walk home with only the birds and the occasional bleat from a sheep in a nearby field for company. She strolled past fields and picked blackberries along the side of the road. She had never tasted wild blackberries. Their flavour and juiciness surprised her. They were so different from the shop bought ones her mother gave her when she was young. Wiping the juice that trickled down her chin, she took the single-track lane that led past their cottage. The road was always quiet, apart from a tractor or two from the farm where the lane came to an end. The only other building for miles. She marvelled at the patterns of dappled sunlight on the broken tarmac as it shone through the branches above her. Stopping a moment to look up through the trees, she watched the branches gently swaying in the breeze. Mornings like these were created to make the world feel better again.

Suddenly feeling chilly in the shade of the trees, Eleanor resumed her walk, longing to reach the open landscape again and emerge back into the sunshine. Here was the only point for miles where trees grew in a cluster, creating a couple of acres of wooded area that the road cut through. The lane curved left, right, and then another sharp left before Eleanor came face to face with Black Spot Bridge. She had passed it in the car several times but had never given it any thought. Now, the hazard tape that stretched across the opening intrigued her. She crept closer, almost expecting to see the remains of old Fred's wrecked car still lying in the river. But there was just sunlight sparkling on the water below. Closer still, she peered over the edge and down into the river beneath her. Boulders jutted out sporadically among thick bushes that covered the bank. The opposite bank was a gentler slope, where the woods continued, following the river downstream before petering out into a dip behind the next field. The warm spring had left the river low, trickling gently over the rocks and stones of the riverbed.

Suddenly, the vision of a skidding car came into her head. Voices screaming at the certainty of death. It wasn't the voice of the car's passenger she could hear, but of Nick and Chris. Her family. As she had heard them so often in her nightmares. She backed away from the edge of the precipice and tried to force the image out of her head. She spun abruptly and ran until the bridge was out of sight and far behind her. Longing to reach the sunlight.

A few minutes later, her heart thumping hard from the exertion, Eleanor slowed as the lane gently rose. When she reached the crest of the hill, she glimpsed her new home through a gap in a high hedge. Sinister and brooding. Almost hidden by brambles and overgrown shrubs in the front garden. She couldn't even see the path they had cut away that led to the front door. The top heavy house leaned to one side and looked as though it was about to topple at any moment. Thoughts of a witch's cottage came to mind, hidden from the outside world. She could easily understand how ghost stories had come about. Even when it was standing in glorious sunlight, she still had a feeling of foreboding. She wasn't ready to return yet.

From her higher vantage point, Eleanor saw a bus travelling towards the village. A day in Northwood Gate could be just what she needed. She'd call Darryl at lunchtime and arrange for him to pick her up after work and bring her home. All thoughts of the house pushed aside, she cut across a field towards the main road.

~

'Darryl, Darryl!'

Darryl, shaken from his thoughts, stopped scraping at the mosaic tiles beneath him. His friend and colleague, Larry, stood a metre above him on the temporary path specially laid for visitors that ran down the side of their trench. The mosaic, only recently discovered, was still in the early stages of excavation.

'A little preoccupied today, are we?' Larry gave a nervous laugh. 'I just wanted to let you know I'm getting a coffee before I start. Do you want one?'

'I'm sorry,' Darryl said. 'Things on my mind.'

'I have to admit, I must have called you half a dozen times. What's up? Did Eleanor find another rat this morning?' Larry pushed his fair hair back out of his eyes, fighting against the wind that blew much stronger here in the open field than closer to the main archaeological site.

Darryl let out a short laugh. The discovery of a rat or two did seem to be a common topic of conversation.

'No, not this time. This time it was a body.'

'A b—' Larry sat heavily on the edge of the path, his legs dangling down across the mud bank at the side of the trench. He gave up trying to keep his long fringe out of his eyes. 'A body? I'm guessing not—'

'No, not a Roman. She found a body buried under our patio.'

'No wonder you're preoccupied. Why on earth did you come in today? I think a body in the garden deserves a day or two off.'

'You know me. I like to work, keep myself busy.'

Larry tried to stifle a laugh.

'There's nothing like living in a cliche,' he said in answer to Darryl's quizzical look. 'The perfect way to spend your Wednesday. Personally, I prefer to take things a little easier on my days off. But, each to their own, as they say.'

Darryl had to admit it was amusing. 'Believe it or not, that's not what's actually bothering me, though.'

Larry, intrigued, slid under the barrier and down onto the mosaic floor, carefully making sure his multicoloured waistcoat didn't come into contact with the earth. He joined Darryl, sitting on the cleared tiles, and out of the wind.

Darryl explained the situation with Eleanor's wedding ring while Larry listened patiently.

'I can't do anything about the body,' Darryl went on. 'Or the house. We're working on it, but it's going to take time. I swear she's nearly at the end of her tether, though, and I want to do something for her now. But I don't know what I can do. If only people would keep their noses out of our business.'

'And what makes you think that'll ever happen?' Larry said, shrugging his shoulders. 'Unrealistic expectations. That's your problem.'

'No, my problem is how bad she feels when busy-bodies interfere and her ring giving them the perfect excuse to do just that.'

'You're not going to want to hear this but, I'd forget about it if I were you,' Larry said meekly. 'Put bluntly, it's her problem, not yours. You can't save the entire world, no matter how hard you want to.'

Darryl liked Larry. He was a good friend, but also a confirmed bachelor. When it came to conversations about relationships, he was of no help.

'You could—' Larry broke off and pressed his lips together firmly, stifling a laugh. 'You could chain her to the kitchen sink.'

Darryl was used to Larry's sense of humour, but was struggling to see the relevance this time.

'That'd solve all your problems. Give her a nice ball and chain, like all good housewives need. At least then she wouldn't be able to find anymore bodies in your garden. Or rats around the house, for that matter.'

Darryl laughed too, though more at Larry's red face as he tried to hold back his laughter than at his effort at humour. Darryl was grateful for the reprieve, though. The laugh was a welcome relief.

'Where's my coffee?' Darryl asked after a couple of minutes.

Larry jumped up like a naughty schoolboy. Brushing off the mud from his knee-length, baggy shorts, he climbed out of the trench and back into the wind.

'I can't save the world, but I think I can do something for Eleanor,' Darryl whispered to himself as he watched Larry trot across to the site's tea-room. His shoulders were still visibly juddering from his laughter. His friend's quip had given Darryl an idea. All he needed now was time to get to a jeweller's.

∼

From the moment Eleanor sank into her seat on the bus, she relaxed. She ambled past views of green, splashed with colourful blossoms for the following hour.

Growing up in the suburbs, her home had been on an ordinary housing estate. Built out of necessity with no thought given to beauty or any kind of aesthetics. Practicality was the need. The only greenery was her own back garden. This current expanse of countryside only brought feelings of isolation and loneliness at first. But it didn't take long for her to relax and appreciate the beauty.

Once in Northwood Gate town, she ambled through the narrow streets sided with quaint lopsided timber buildings, and took pleasure in noting points of interest she'd learnt. The difference between close studding timber work and half-timbered. The difference between a gargoyle and a grotesque. Since meeting Darryl, she had learnt so much, though not always willingly. It was interesting, but her enthusiasm didn't quite match his.

Lunchtime came quicker than expected and Eleanor stopped at a busy tea-room. She was lucky to find the last available table, seating only two, but perfect for her. Tucked at the back of the room, she sat facing the window, watching life. The tourists wandering aimlessly, the frustrated locals being held up by those tourists in their busy day-to-day lives. Each one wrapped in their own story. Her story was being cooped up in a house of horrors. A prison-like situation where all she had to think about was the house, or rather the problems with the house. The town brought her back to reality. Even her concerns and worries about Darryl keeping secrets seemed laughable now.

Relaxing in her chair, Eleanor gazed around her, taking in the low, characterful beams that crisscrossed the ceiling and the large old bread oven in the side wall. The tea-room made the most of its quaint ambience. Black and white photographs dotted the walls, framed in dark wood that matched the distinctive beams, and one picture in particular caught her attention.

Rushmere cottage, their house. Not rundown and melancholy as it looked now, but immaculate and dignified.

Taken before the neglect, before the rodents had taken over, and presumably, before the murder. Darryl had been right in his musings. It will be beautiful.

'Can I take your order?' a cheerful voice said.

Eleanor jolted from her reverie. A woman stood at her side with a pen and notepad in hand. Hot and flustered, her face and demeanour were friendly and open; thriving on the hard work of a busy lunchtime.

'I'm sorry,' Eleanor said. 'I had lost myself in one of your old photographs.'

'Rushmere cottage?' the woman said, looking in the direction Eleanor had been staring so intently.

'Yes,' Eleanor replied. 'It's a shame it doesn't look like that now.'

'You know it?'

'I live there now,' Eleanor said with an enormous sigh.

The woman's friendly smile became fixed. 'That's nice,' she said. 'What can I get for you?' Her cheery voice had become blunt, though cracking with polite intentions. In an instant, she became old and tired. Eleanor, unable to ask what she had said wrong, stuttered her order for an omelette and salad.

The woman left hastily. Eleanor's eyes followed her till she disappeared through a doorway to the kitchen area. News of Miss Starling's body could have been known locally by now. Especially with people like Stella around. Immediately, Eleanor's imagination went into overdrive. Maybe this woman had some connection. She looked scared. Maybe she had already known about the body in the garden. Known before Eleanor had found it. *Stop it,* Eleanor chastised herself. *She could just as well of had designs on buying the place herself and had been saving for the last umpteen years.*

She changed her focus to a scene on the wall next to the kitchen doorway. It was the same view she had seen that morning as she'd stood outside the village shop, though the spring scene of this morning was one of summer in the photograph. The trees dotted around the village green were full of foliage, and the flower beds were overflowing in what would have been spectacular summer colours if the picture hadn't been black and white. She gazed around the tea-room searching for more images she recognised and soon realised Bramblemere must have appealed to the photographer. So many images of beauty and tranquillity.

Eleanor's order arrived in silence. She bit her lip, torn between guilt and curiosity. Had she upset her, or was this woman the cause of Miss Starling's demise? *Stop it.* She occupied herself with searching through the photographs while she ate, with only the occasional surreptitious glance towards the crazy lady, as Eleanor had now named her. A girl in her late teens, who was in many of the photographs, drew her attention. An attractive girl with subtle features and large round eyes. No make-up or jewellery other than small ear studs. She was clearly a favourite with the photographer, as she appeared so frequently. Some scenes at a distance, such as sitting by the village pond, others close up. But always easily recognisable by her distinctive waist length, dark hair.

A different waitress arrived to remove Eleanor's plate. The girl had dyed blue hair and a ring through her nose. A stark contrast to the quaint antiquated ambience of the tea-room. Eleanor asked for a coffee and sat back, relishing her day of freedom and enjoying a new vision of Bramblemere.

When the girl returned with Eleanor's coffee, curiosity consumed her. 'Do you know who the girl is in these photos?' Eleanor asked. 'The one with the waist length hair? She was obviously popular with the photographer.'

'That's Mum,' the girl said. 'Grandma was a keen photographer, as you can see, and it certainly doesn't look like Mum objected. Not then, anyway. Now she's not so keen on them. She wants to take them down, but I won't let her. It's my way of torturing her,' she added in a whisper. 'You've got to torture your mum, right?'

The waitress turned to leave but double-backed hesitantly and said, 'Mum said you're from Rushmere cottage.'

The fame that came with being the new owners of the cottage startled Eleanor. 'Yes, yes, I am. I hope I didn't upset your mum,' Eleanor continued. 'When she found out I live there, she—'

'Don't worry about it,' the girl interrupted, hugging her tray in front of her. 'Bad memories make her a bit sensitive. A friend of hers came in this morning and told her about - about what's been found,' she said with a semblance of tactfulness. 'Granddad was the detective investigating the disappearance. Apparently, everyone thought it was an open and shut case. But he - well, to be honest, I don't know. It all happened before I was born, but I do know that it was around that time when he walked out. Couldn't handle the stress of it all, and not the happiest of marriages. He just left Mum and Grandma and never looked back. Mum still finds it hard to deal with.'

'I'm so sorry,' Eleanor said. Her words inadequate for her guilt at thinking the worst of this poor woman.

'Would you like to see her?' the girl asked excitedly. 'Miss Starling, I mean. She was another of Grandma's favourites.'

Eleanor sat stunned at the invitation. The girl took her silence for affirmation and pointed to one of the photos on the wall directly behind Eleanor. The photograph was of a beautiful young woman. Her face turned to the sunlight, revelling in the warmth. Her, what Eleanor took for blonde hair in the black-and-white picture, was gently wafting from her face, revealing a long slender neck, with a slight scar behind her ear that ordinarily would have been hidden by her hair.

'The image is really grainy because Grandma took it at a distance. The story goes, she didn't like having her photograph taken, so Grandma sneaked a lot of them, but never put them up. Not until a few weeks after she had disappeared, anyway. There's several of her in here. I think Mum might've got a bit jealous, and that's the real reason she wants to take them all down.' She smothered a laugh before continuing, 'Personally, I think the grainy effect adds grit to the simple image. Turning something ethereal into something real, rather than looking like she's made of plastic.'

The girl shivered as though an icy chill had gone down her back.

'I'm studying photography at college,' the girl added apologetically. 'I guess it runs in the family.'

At that moment, a group of five who had been sitting at the table next to Eleanor got up and left.

'This is another of my favourites,' the girl said, pulling Eleanor's focus to another photograph that had been on the wall behind the large party.

Miss Starling was with a small child on the village green. Eleanor recognised the pond behind them. The woman had crouched down to the child's level, and they were laughing together, playing a clapping game from what Eleanor could tell. The girl beckoned Eleanor closer to the image. Eleanor left her coffee on the table, her knees almost giving way, and hesitantly made her way to the photograph.

'You can really feel the connection between them, can't you? Such a joyful moment caught forever,' the girl continued.

'Marie,' a voice called from the kitchen.

'Got to go,' the girl said and trotted back to the kitchen, leaving Eleanor staring at a woman full of life and loved by those around her. It soon became unbearable, and Eleanor returned to focus on her coffee. Miss Starling was no longer just a pile of bones.

Eleanor sipped at her coffee and watched intently out the window. Claustrophobic from the photographs of Miss Starling surrounding her, her heart lifted when she saw Darryl walking along the street on the opposite side of the road, finishing a sandwich. She made to leave, wanting to surprise him, but then he turned into the shop opposite. A jewellery shop. Her heart was suddenly in her throat. The last time she had gone into a jeweller's was with her husband-to-be, Nick, to buy their wedding rings. Subconsciously reaching for her ring, her fingers began twisting it. Round and round.

Darryl had made it known that he understood how much Stella's not-so-subtle glances towards her ring had upset her this morning. She guessed that, for Darryl, the easiest solution would be to replace it. Replace it with a ring of his own.

They had only known each other for a few months. Buying a house together had been a big enough step, and maybe that had been too fast. There was no denying their relationship was good. There was always something more between them, something only two people who had fought for their lives together could understand. But marriage? Not to mention the disloyalty to Nick that rose in her stomach.

4

Eleanor stayed in her seat and waited, watching the door to the jewellers where Darryl had disappeared.

"Call me at lunchtime," she remembered him saying. His last words to her before he had driven off that morning. She rifled through her bag for her phone, almost dropping it in her haste.

'Hi, how are you feeling after your walk?' he said on answering.

'OK,' she tried to sound normal, though her hands were trembling. 'Were you late for work this morning?'

'No, luckily the traffic wasn't too bad. I sailed through.'

'Where are you now?' she said, though immediately regretted it.

She didn't want to make him suspicious, but she needed to know if he would tell her the truth. Her fist clenched at the slight pause before his answer.

'Just sat at the site having some lunch.'

Eleanor floundered as she held back tears. He was lying to her.

'You? Are you home yet?' he went on.

'No, not yet. I got a bit carried away with the whole out-for-a-walk idea.' She forced some high-spirited cheer into her voice. 'Will you be straight home after work?'

'Of course,' he said with a slight laugh.

Again, Eleanor regretted her question. His voice was strained. He was getting suspicious.

'Why? Is there something you want me to pick up from town?'

'No, not at all. I just wondered.'

She wanted to keep him on the line, give him more of a chance to explain, even though logic told her he wouldn't. A surprise proposal. That was a secret worth keeping. But it wasn't a surprise Eleanor wanted. An awkward silence followed. She thought she had better get off the phone before she asked any more stupid questions. He didn't seem too keen to be on the phone himself.

'I'll see you later, then.' Eleanor finally gave in. There was nothing more to say.

'Sure. Take things easy this afternoon, OK?'

'Yeah, I thought I might get the bus into town.'

Darryl's laugh sounded stilted on the other end of the line. 'It's a long journey on the bus. Wait till tomorrow and I can run you in.'

'Maybe,' Eleanor replied. 'I'll leave you to your lunch, then.'

'OK, see you later,' and the call ended.

Contrived and uncomfortable.

Eleanor continued watching from the tea-room. A few minutes later Darryl stepped out of the jeweller's, looking up and down the street, a small plastic bag in his hand. He returned the way he came. Was he looking suspicious, or was it just in Eleanor's head? Overwhelming nausea kept her in her seat. She took her time, breathing deep and slow. The last thing she wanted to do was to vomit in the middle of the tea-room.

Darryl was having second thoughts as he drove home from work. He had been so sure all morning that it was the right thing to do and was excited about the prospect of the perfect solution. There was no denying Eleanor's reaction to the events in the village shop that morning, but how could he help? Then the answer had come to him after his conversation with Larry. He had even taken time out of his lunch break to drive into Northwood Gate town centre and visit the jewellers.

With no time to stop and eat, Darryl had finished his sandwich en route before entering the jewellers. An elderly man rose from behind the counter, eager for the custom. His plush, red chair now seated his book, the spine broken as it lay open, faced down. He pulled his wire-framed glasses to the end of his nose and peered over them as he stood with his hands clasped in front of him. His grey hair neatly combed in a side parting and stuck to the sides of his head with thickly applied hair product. A smart, dark-grey waistcoat and blue chequered bowtie finished his antiquated appearance.

Darryl was perusing over a selection the salesman had suggested when Eleanor had called and interrupted. The man did little to hide his impatience. Mobile phones were nothing more than a nuisance in this modern age. Not wanting to let on to Eleanor, Darryl tried to continue the conversation as normal while the salesperson had folded his arms and stared disdainfully at Darryl over the top of his glasses. A distraction he could have done without.

But now, on his way home, Darryl wasn't sure how to go about presenting his gift to Eleanor, or whether he should at all. They had never spoken about her still wearing her wedding ring. It had never been an issue until that morning.

His phone rang, interrupting his thoughts. He glanced down

at it on the seat beside him. Rachel. She had rung a couple of times during the day and each time he had avoided it. He left it ringing and continued driving home. What could his ex-wife possibly want from him? The only thing they had in common now were their twin girls, Kathy and Alex, who were both happy at university together. If it was urgent, Rachel would have to leave a message. She never did, so he assumed it couldn't be important. But Rachel being Rachel let it ring, and then she'd ring again later. She always knew how to annoy him.

He turned his focus back to Eleanor. She was his priority now. It was clear she was struggling with the house renovation project. He could understand that the place may look horrific, but it was mostly superficial. The structural engineer had already inspected the house, including that ten-foot crack that Eleanor was stressing about, and it was all under control. The best thing in their favour was that somehow the house had escaped being listed. No hoops to jump through for building consents from Historic England.

But then, finding a body in the garden was the worst thing that could have happened. And maybe he should have mentioned about the ghost stories before she heard them from someone else. He had always intended to; it was one of those things he had never got around to. There wasn't much he could do about it now, but he may have an answer for her wedding ring. Self-doubt trickled in again as his phone went silent. Coming across as pushy wouldn't be good. He had no problem with her wearing the ring. She clearly wanted to continue wearing it, so maybe they should carry on the way they were. What business was it of anybody else? All she needed to say was that she was widowed. A car accident. It's partly true. OK, maybe not. A car crash, then.

Darryl turned into the gravel driveway that ran down the side of the house. He took the small jewellery box from its bag and sat staring at it. Still uncertain whether to give it to her, he placed it in his inside jacket pocket. *I'll see how things go. If it's the right time, then it's the right time.*

His phone rang again. Rachel. He took pleasure in declining the call.

~

Eleanor stiffened at the sound of the car pulling onto the gravel driveway. A sound she had got used to over the last few weeks, synonymous with Darryl returning from work and the pleasure that thought had afforded. But not today.

She had left the tea-room and caught the bus back to Bramblemere. Thinking of everything and nothing at once. The walk home from the bus stop had been fast and determined, the pleasurable amble of that morning long forgotten. Once home, her nerves wouldn't let her settle. Moving from one job to another, finishing none. Two hours of cleaning, washing, tidying, before returning to the cleaning again and continuing the cycle over again. All the time avoiding the garden. Safer to stay indoors.

The sound of the gravel stopped her mid-way through cleaning one of the kitchen cupboards. Baking trays and saucepans strewn across the floor. Her nerves intensified any noise, and even the silence as the car engine switched off. The creak of the car door as it opened and slammed. Footsteps crunched on the gravel, moving round the house and towards the small garden gate. The hinges squeaked open. A drawn-out screech before it clicked shut again. There was no sound on the grassy path that led from the gate to the back door, but his footsteps pounded in her head like those of a giant coming to crush her. As he came closer, Eleanor shook herself back to reality, quickly gathered up her cleaning supplies, and ran out of the kitchen. *Stay out of his way,* she thought. *Don't give him the chance to propose.*

'Eleanor,' she heard him call.

She reprimanded herself for not being quicker at leaving the room.

'In the middle of cleaning the bathroom,' she called back and kept on moving.

'And the kitchen, so it would seem,' she heard Darryl say. His voice growing distant as she pounded up the stairs.

In the bathroom, she scrubbed at the detergent that she had left covering the bath to do its work. It was only a few moments later that Darryl arrived at the bathroom doorway.

'Did you have a good day?' he asked.

'Yes, thanks.' Eleanor kept her head down, almost hidden as she scrubbed the inside of the bath. Far too busy for conversation. She kept odd sentences to a minimum, her answers to questions were short and blunt.

'Where did you end up going?' Darryl persevered.

'Oh, here and there.'

'I bet your feet ache.' He leaned casually against the door frame.

Eleanor caught his laid back attitude out of the corner of her eye. Her shocked pause didn't seem to give him any cause for concern. 'They're fine,' she spat.

'Eleanor?' Darryl's voice had changed to a soft, enquiring tone. 'Is everything OK?'

'Yes, of course.' Eleanor subconsciously held her breath. Should she ask him about his visit to the jewellery shop? This was her opportunity to find out the truth. Or should she wait to see if he tells her of his own accord? 'Why shouldn't it be?' she replied, unable to bring herself to ask the question. Scared of knowing the truth.

'I feel like I'm walking on eggshells. Have I done something wrong?'

'I don't know, have you?' She finally stopped scrubbing and looked up at Darryl. This was it. This was his chance.

'Not that I know of.'

'Good, well then, that's settled.' Eleanor returned to scrubbing the bath with renewed enthusiasm.

Finally, Darryl left to change into clean clothes, leaving her quietly seething.

Cooking the dinner, she continued to ignore him as much as possible, although now it was because she was angry with him for not explaining his trip. Eating dinner was more difficult. They were using the large, formal dining room as their bedroom, as they could not use the bedrooms upstairs. The dining table, therefore, was squeezed to one side of the kitchen, pushed against one of the uneven walls. Sitting in such close proximity, Eleanor's last tactic would not work. She thought about keeping him talking about other things. She longed to tell him of the photographs she had seen of Miss Starling, but then she would have to admit to being in the tea-room, which would create more questions. Questions she didn't want to face. Instead, it was time to ask the questions and keep him talking about his day. He usually enjoyed that anyway.

'How was work?' Eleanor started. 'Uncover anything exciting today?'

'Only terrible memories of how infuriating kids can be,' Darryl said. 'We had a school party on site today, but once the holidays start, it'll be hell.'

'What happened?' and that was the last she said for some time.

Darryl enthused about children putting their fingers where they shouldn't, and the so-called responsible adults with them that didn't seem to care. Eleanor, tense and on edge throughout.

It wasn't until near the end of the meal, with only a few mouthfuls left, that he said, 'I was thinking today about something that was said at the village shop this morning.' He pulled out his chair as though about to stand.

Eleanor's throat tightened, and she gripped her knife and fork with much more force than was necessary. Her mind went blank as she struggled to find something to change the subject. Darryl fidgeted a little in his seat and then tucked himself back under the table.

'Mrs Stuck-up Stella,' he said, pulling a face, 'mentioned the teaching assistant had gone into labour early and the school was having trouble finding someone to cover for the next few weeks.'

'I remember,' Eleanor breathed out the words in relief, not realising she had been holding her breath.

'You could help,' Darryl went on. 'You used to be a teacher, so you know the ropes, and I thought it might help to get you out of the house, even if only for a couple of weeks. What do you think?'

Eleanor couldn't speak. Her entire body had gone numb. Memories of her son, Chris, had sprung into her head. He had only been five years old at the time of his death. She couldn't return to her old job of teaching after that. The memories would have been devastating. Could she return now, though? In truth, the thought made her sick. She shook her head. Just a small motion, but vigorous.

'I can't,' she whispered.

Thankfully, Darryl didn't push it and they ended the meal in silence.

~

That evening Darryl and Eleanor relaxed on the sofa watching TV. The lounge had soon become their favourite room in the house. Large enough to accommodate two sofas with ample room to spare yet still keeping a country cottage feel, while joking that the stone inglenook fireplace was large enough to be a room of its own. At the end of the day, they could close themselves away into this one room and forget about all their other worries. Cosy, warm and safe.

Darryl quietly looked down on Eleanor as she lay sleeping on the sofa, tucked under a thick green blanket and her head on his lap. A semblance of normality. With his arm across her, he watched the muscles in her face twitch, small subconscious movements, while he paid no attention to the film they were supposed to be watching. He still regretted mentioning the school job, there had been mostly silence since. He had initially intended to present her gift. He had even begun to retrieve it from his pocket before those thoughts of self-doubt returned. She had been in a strange mood all evening. Her walk from the village that morning clearly hadn't helped to settle her nerves. Though changing the subject to the school hadn't helped. Now she hardly spoke to him at all. He had hoped that a good time would arise during the evening for his proposition, but he had a distinct feeling that he had ruined that possibility. So, the box stayed in his jacket pocket. For now, it was best to stay quiet.

Darryl jumped, shaken from his thoughts at the sound of a door slamming on the television. The bang woke Eleanor with a start too, but it only took seconds before she settled down and began watching the film. A few moments later, she sat up suddenly.

'Switch off the TV,' she whispered.

Darryl looked at her curiously.

'Quick, switch it off,' she repeated.

She had given no explanation, and he sat bewildered. She reached over him, grabbed the remote with force, and turned it off herself.

The sun had not set when they had first sat. The light had faded with the evening, leaving the only light from the television itself. Now, with the television off, they sat in darkness.

'What are you doing?' he said.

'I heard something.' Her voice still a whisper.

'What?'

'I don't know, that's why I want it quiet in case I hear it again,' she growled at him.

Darryl bit his lip. His first thoughts were of the wind, rats, old plumbing, or any number of other things that creaked and groaned in the house every night and had never bothered her before. But he knew better than to say anything.

A creaking sound from upstairs broke the silence. Darryl bolted upright.

'That was a floorboard,' he said.

'More to the point, what would make a floorboard creak like that?' Eleanor stood and marched towards the door.

Darryl followed. 'Not a rat, that's for sure.'

5

Crossing the hallway, Darryl jumped as a door slammed upstairs and Eleanor let out an eek of a scream. A thump came from outside, at the back of the house, followed by a clatter from upstairs. His nerves heightened, he wondered about those ghost stories. He didn't believe in spirits, but he had never been face to face with anything supernatural, either. In the cold light of day, it was easy to say ghosts didn't exist, but now, in the dark? Strange noises upstairs? And in a house that would have seen more than its fair share of deaths over the years, let alone the one of more recent times. It was enough to make anyone have second thoughts. Light was what he needed. At least eliminating the darkness was one thing he could do to help ease the tension, and he flicked on the light switch. The noise outside had created a moment of indecision, but it only took a second to recognise that what was inside the house was of a higher priority than outside.

'Stay here,' he whispered to Eleanor, leaving her at the entrance to the lounge. Worried that this could push her over the edge.

He turned back towards the stairs. Before he completed his

first step, he jumped again at a knocking sound. Someone was knocking on their front door. Darryl motioned for Eleanor to stay where she was as he moved to open it. Hesitantly, he pulled the large oak door open, letting out an audible sigh at the sight of DCI Hanson standing on the doorstep.

'Good evening, Mr Westwood,' the DCI said. 'Just thought I'd pop round and see how the two of you are. Mrs Garrett seemed very shaken yesterday.'

'Good timing,' Darryl whispered. The DCI's words washing over him. 'Someone's in the house.' No need to mention anything about ghosts.

Eleanor moved to Darryl's side. Her face, pale.

The police officer's manner changed immediately from the local friendly bobby to the investigator in charge.

'Tell me what's happened,' he said sternly.

'I heard noises upstairs,' Eleanor explained.

'And then out back,' Darryl continued. At that moment, a loud thump came from upstairs. 'They're still here.'

'Wait here,' DCI Hanson said and crept slowly up the stairs, though if his intention had been to be quiet, it was pointless. Each step creaked at the slightest movement.

When the DCI was almost at the top, a movement startled Darryl over his shoulder as Eleanor moved past and followed DCI Hanson. Her light steps carried her quickly up the stairs.

'Eleanor,' he called quietly, but she didn't turn back. After a moment's hesitation, he followed her. Surely it was best to all stay together.

He could hear soft shuffling noises coming from one of the back bedrooms as he moved further up the stairs. DCI Hanson and Eleanor were already at the door and he hurried to join them. The officer turned the handle and slowly opened the door an inch. The room was in darkness. Darryl's hands trembled, and he balled them into fists to stop them shaking as the DCI pushed the door open further. A plume of dust and soot swept through the doorway, trailing the frantically beating wings of a bird.

Eleanor screamed at the sudden outburst as the bird came straight towards her, flailing her arms frantically to protect herself.

The officer let out an audible sigh. 'Just a pigeon. Flown down the chimney by the look of it.'

Darryl pulled Eleanor close, protecting her from the commotion, though the poor bird seemed as startled as Eleanor, leaving a trail of soot across the landing floor as it swept through.

'Then it was a pigeon with heavy feet to cause our floorboards to creak,' Darryl said.

Showing intrigue, DCI Hanson entered the room, and Eleanor followed. Darryl was pulled along too as he kept a protective arm around her.

The room was full of boxes. Some old, some new, but most now covered in soot. One was lying on its side. Papers scattered across the floor.

'This will be what made the thump,' Eleanor said as she drew herself away from Darryl and lifted the box back to the top of its pile, though she changed her mind when she saw the box beneath was collapsing in on itself. It wouldn't have taken much for the one above it to have fallen. She turned, not knowing what to do with it. There was no empty space, so instead, she dumped it back on the floor where it had fallen. But at least now it was upright. They would just have to step over it. Thankfully, the box contained nothing breakable. Paperwork mostly, and luckily, Darryl had collected up the scattered papers. A draft wafted across her face and looking around the room, she suddenly realised something wasn't right.

'The window's open,' she said with surprise. She strode across the room to look out but could see nothing but black.

'If you're anything like us, we're always forgetting to close the windows,' DCI Hanson joked.

'No, we don't come in here. As you can see, the place is just storage at the moment.' She forced away her thoughts of annoyance at having a house where only the minimum number of rooms were available to use. 'We always keep this window closed. I'm certain of it. The only room we use up here at the moment is the bathroom,' Eleanor went on as she turned to the window and slammed it shut, annoyed with more problems. Then something outside caught her eye.

'There's a light in the garden,' she exclaimed.

Both Darryl and the DCI joined her at the window.

'Look, someone's there with a torch.'

'I'll get him.' Darryl immediately turned to run.

'No, Sir,' The DCI called after him. 'They may be dangerous. Leave it to me.'

He pulled Darryl back and left at a run. The sound of his feet pounded on the bare floorboards as he ran across the landing, down the stairs, and finally disappeared as he double-backed along the hall to the kitchen and the back door. While she listened, Eleanor watched the light from the window. Whoever it was must have heard the commotion inside, for they had started running. She watched the jumping motion of the small beam of light as it moved further away. DCI Hanson emerged from the house and chased after it. Eleanor was left bemused in the silence. Darryl stood behind her, peering over the top of her head and watching the events outside. His hands placed protectively on her shoulders.

The torchlight was soon out of sight, and DCI Hanson was nowhere to be seen. A sound behind them pulled their focus, and they turned back to the room, coming face to face with the pigeon, apparently still hunting for its way out. Eleanor quickly reopened the window, and they both ducked as it swooped over them and out into the night. She closed the window again and watched as it flew into the darkness.

'Didn't think pigeons were nocturnal,' Darryl mumbled.

But Eleanor ignored him. She had other questions on her mind, but questions she couldn't speak to Darryl about. She couldn't admit that she had been in the tea-room that day. That she had learnt more about Miss Starling and the impact of her disappearance.

'Do you think he'll catch them?' she asked instead.

'Don't know, he seemed keen enough to get out there and try, that's for sure.'

He sounded as dazed as Eleanor felt.

'Why would somebody do this?' Her voice quivered as she fought back her anger.

'I don't know,' he said, gently enveloping her in his arms. 'But I would certainly like to find out.'

Eleanor, facing the window, gazed out into the night. Clouds covered the sky, hiding the moon. Her pale reflection stared back at her. But in her mind, it was Miss Starling's face she saw. Pale and scared.

Darryl gently kissed the top of Eleanor's head and left her, moving towards another part of the room. Her eyes watched unseeing as he collected some papers he had missed from earlier. Questions ran round her head. Questions of Miss Starling, of the kind of person who could have killed her. Of the kind of person who could torment them like this.

After a few minutes of silence, a knock sounded at the front door again. DCI Hanson stood rosy-cheeked and sweaty from the chase.

'I'm sorry,' he gasped. 'They got away.'

Eleanor invited him in and fetched some water to help cool him and ease his dry throat.

'Did you see who it was?' asked Darryl impatiently.

'No, someone fast, that's for sure. Probably one of the kids from town, thinking it's funny to try and scare the new people who have moved into the local haunted house. You can imagine this place has been a bit of a magnet for mischievous teenagers over the years.'

'That would explain the pile of cigarette ends that were in the garden when we first moved in,' Darryl said. 'Seems quite extreme for a kid to go to, though, just for a bit of fun.'

'Not for kids from town.' DCI Hanson shrugged his shoulders apologetically. 'But this time, they have also trespassed into an ongoing crime scene.'

Eleanor agreed with Darryl. This was more than teenage hormones running wild. This had been planned, and she couldn't imagine a pigeon had just happened by.

'I'll send an officer round in the morning for some more investigation,' DCI Hanson continued, 'but, in the meantime, I'd say just keep an eye out in case they decide to come back. There's not much else we can do right now, I'm afraid.'

'Do you think it's likely,' Eleanor asked, 'that they'll come back?' Kids or not, she didn't fancy another evening like that.

'Who knows what kids will do these days. But hopefully the chase has shaken them up a bit and they'll think twice about trying something like that again.'

'What about Miss Starling? Have you found out anything? I know it hasn't been long, but...' Eleanor ignored Darryl's quizzical look. After their argument that morning, here she was investigating.

The DCI hesitated before answering. 'May I ask where you got that name from?'

'We spoke with your wife this morning, in the village shop,' Eleanor said tentatively.

The DCI closed his eyes in frustration. Eleanor had the feeling it was either that or rolling his eyes, which wouldn't have been very professional, particularly about his own wife.

'We have not yet identified the body,' he said sternly, 'and we are following several lines of enquiry.' He blew out an enormous sigh. 'I will say you don't need to worry yourself about it. Do you still have the card I gave you yesterday? Then if anything like this happens again, please call me. I'm just glad I was here to help.'

They followed the DCI to the front door, where he left them with a cheery nod. Eleanor and Darryl watched as he walked away from the house. His car parked opposite in a small lay-by at the side of the lane.

Eleanor stared out into the darkness as the last glimmer of the car lights disappeared down the lane. Their house was a couple of miles or so outside the village and there were no streetlights or close neighbours. Eleanor could just make out the faint silhouette of the bushes at the end of their garden path, but no further. Just darkness. Everywhere darkness.

'There are a lot of reasons why I could walk away,' she whispered.

Darryl turned to look at her. His arm round her shoulders, he squeezed gently.

'Walk away from this house, I mean,' she clarified. 'But I refuse to be intimidated like this. Why would somebody break in here? This has to be something to do with Miss Starling.'

In truth, she had struggled to get the images from the tea-room photographs out of her mind. How full of life Miss Starling had been, and so loved by the children. Eleanor's imagination filled in the blanks for the rest of her life, leading to how scared she must have been the day she was killed. Earlier that evening, during the film, Eleanor had fallen asleep. Her nightmares pushed into her mind. Buried alive; paralysed as earth was shovelled on top of her. Unable to push the dirt from her face till it was falling down her throat. Suffocating in the darkness. Shaking off the memory, she thought about what she could do to make a difference. What could she do to help herself feel as though she was doing something instead of sitting back and watching it all happen in front of her?

'That job at the school,' she said finally, rallying her courage, 'didn't they say Miss Starling was a teacher there when she went missing? Maybe I *will* ask if they could use my help. Maybe do some investigating of my own while I'm there.'

6

Friday morning, Eleanor gathered everything she would need to volunteer at the school. CV, certificates, etc. She reasoned it was more likely they would take her as a volunteer rather than risk applying for a paid position, only to be turned away because of budget restrictions.

Rummaging through numerous boxes had taken longer than expected. Darryl had left for work over an hour ago and so she needed to make the thirty-minute journey on foot. All morning she had kept her mind focused on practicalities, the necessities of the task ahead. The walk into Bramblemere gave her mind time to roam. She could do the job, no problem, physically and mentally. But emotionally? As she had feared, her night was broken by images of the earth closing in on her. Choking and terrifying screams ringing in her ears. As she came closer to the school, the images changed. Memories of Chris holding her hand; looking up at her with so much love in his eyes, her heart ached.

She reached the school around nine thirty, but found she couldn't go in. Her knees threatening to give way, she lowered herself onto a bench on the village green and stared at the school opposite. It stared back menacingly. The two huge, grand windows, one either side of the door, were the school's wide fixated eyes. The large arched doorway, its mouth ready to swallow her. Sitting on the peaceful village green only intensified what she knew she would find inside. Children. Children playing. Laughing. Breathing. Everything her own child could no longer do. Eleanor screwed her eyes and shut out the stone face, intimidating her from her intention. She had to remember her purpose and focused on the photographs she had seen of Miss Starling. No longer a pile of bones unearthed from her garden. She had been a living soul. She hadn't deserved what had happened to her, the same as Eleanor hadn't deserved to have her husband and son taken from her so cruelly. There was nothing more she could do for them now, but there may be something she could do for Miss Starling. Her nightmares flashing in her head, she opened her eyes and stood resolute.

'It'll only be for a couple of weeks. You can cope with that. Let's face it, you've coped with a lot worse.' She said the words out loud, but they did not convince her.

Eleanor marched across the green and through the open doorway into the school reception area before any more doubts could seep their way in.

'Good morning, I was wondering if I may be able to help you,' she said with as much confidence as she could muster.

The woman behind the reception desk listened while Eleanor told how she had heard that one of their teaching assistants had gone into labour early. She explained how she used to be a primary school teacher and was happy to help in any way she could. Handing over her paperwork, she made a joke about needing to get out of the house and just a couple of weeks helping in the school would really help with her sanity.

A laugh came from a man standing to one side, briefly distracting her. She had taken no notice of the man till now. He was tall, smart, and austere looking. She acknowledged his laugh and smiled politely.

The secretary looked down at Eleanor's paperwork. 'Rushmere cottage?' The secretary said with intrigue. Eleanor turned back towards her. The woman's face had turned pale, almost matching her grey hair.

'Well, no wonder you want to get out of the house.' The man joined in the conversation.

'You know the place?' Eleanor asked, bobbing her head between the two.

'The entire village does, especially after the recent discovery there. The truth of the mysterious disappearance of Miss Starling,' he said, as though reading the title of an Agatha Christie novel. 'Susan,' he continued, addressing the secretary. 'You must have known Miss Starling.'

The secretary, Susan, nodded briefly before turning back to her computer.

'She used to work here, you know,' the man continued.

Eleanor reacted as though she didn't know. 'It must have come as quite a shock to you,' Eleanor said towards Susan, determined to begin her investigation as soon as possible.

'Yes, well, of course, we don't yet know for certain that it is Miss Starling,' the secretary said without turning from her computer.

'Oh, I think we can safely assume it is,' the tall man declared. 'And if you're anything like my wife, then yes. Yes, it did come as a shock. I'm afraid Susan doesn't like to get involved in idle tittle-tattle.'

'You say it came as a shock to your wife, too?' Eleanor asked, making a mental note that she will need to find a way in to Susan's trusted circle. Everybody has something they like to talk about and Eleanor needed to find it before she was going to be able to get Susan to open up.

'My wife knew her too,' the man continued with enthusiasm, 'probably better than anyone. Miss Starling was a teacher here at the time she went missing, you see, and my wife was her TA,' he said, proud of this connection. 'I can imagine how you must feel a need to remove yourself from the vicinity of the shallow grave, so to speak. Will Cowley,' he announced. 'Headteacher of this establishment,' he said, shaking Eleanor's hand.

He turned his attention to the secretary. 'Susan, could you do the necessary checks for Mrs...?' He turned back to Eleanor.

Eleanor hesitated. Should she be Mrs, Miss or even Ms? Should she be Garrett or use her maiden name, Dowling?

But in the split second it took to think, Susan stated, 'Mrs Garrett,' reading her name from her CV.

Eleanor hadn't changed the name. Too many other things had been on her mind to even consider it.

'Just Eleanor,' she said in a friendly manner.

'Well, Eleanor, you may be our guardian angel and, my word, we can certainly make use of your skills. Let me show you round our school.'

Leaving her bag at reception, Will Cowley showed Eleanor the classrooms, the hall, the school field and playground, moving from one end of the school to the other. Each class was just as she had expected. Children's work, bright and colourful, covered the walls. The large windows that looked so menacing to her from the outside let the light shine brightly into the rooms. The last classroom was for the reception children, where he introduced her to Becky, his wife. She was smaller than Eleanor by two or three inches, with a friendly face and a large, beaming smile.

'Mrs Eleanor Garrett has kindly offered her services as your assistant for the next couple of weeks. I'm sure you won't object.'

'No, not at all. That's very — oh. Of course. You must — please excuse me.' A child had been pulling on Becky's trouser leg. She crouched down and spoke gently with the child and then sent him back to his table. She turned back to Eleanor.

'Sorry about that, but that's children for you.'

Another child came dancing round their legs, dressed as a pirate.

Images of Chris in his own pirate costume flashed into Eleanor's head. Swashbuckling his way through their lounge.

'That's a very generous offer,' Becky said.

But Eleanor's head was spinning, her body had gone numb.

'Can you start now? The sooner the better, as far as I'm concerned. Two days on my own in here is more than enough,' she said, laughing. She stopped the dancing child and directed her back to the dress-up corner where she had come from.

Eleanor's doubts grew with every second. She couldn't do this. She fought for air, her chest aching with the effort to breathe.

Will's laughter boomed. 'Maybe we'll leave it till Monday. We don't want to go scaring Eleanor away before she's even begun.'

After the weekend. That would give her time. Already exhausted from fake smiles and false enthusiasm, Eleanor could prepare herself. *Focus on Miss Starling,* she told herself, as she stood, frozen. *Miss Starling, Miss Starling.*

'I know it's short notice,' Becky said, 'but why don't you and your husband come round for dinner tonight?'

'Well—' Eleanor stammered.

'About seven?' Becky interrupted. 'Then we can have the chance to get to know each other a little better.' She reached for another child, dancing round her legs, tickling her as she continued in a light jovial voice, 'without these pesky children around.'

Mrs Cowley and the child laughed together before she sent the child to her table. Eleanor couldn't help but smile at their fun. She had enjoyed working as a teacher. It was good for her to remember that. It was hard work, but also a lot of fun.

'I was telling Eleanor that you knew the woman she found in her garden,' Will interrupted Eleanor's thoughts.

'Sorry?' Becky whispered, staring at Eleanor. She looked as though she couldn't breathe.

Eleanor had already encountered one person's distress from the news at the tea-room yesterday. She had been so preoccupied with her own concerns that she hadn't thought about how the news might affect those closest to Miss Starling. And now, Eleanor was full of guilt at Becky's reaction.

'Miss Starling. I was telling her you knew Miss Starling in the days of old,' Will said with an aren't-I-amusing tone. 'Of course, I didn't tell you, did I? Eleanor lives at Rushmere cottage now.' He turned to Eleanor and asked, 'Was it actually you that —' he broke from his sentence and peered round for nearby children. Seeing they were all occupied elsewhere, he continued with a whisper, 'found the body?'

'Yes, it was, and I'll thank you not to keep reminding me of it,' Eleanor said with a slight laugh, hoping Will would get the hint. Both for her sake and his wife's. But, apparently not.

'Yes, of course. I understand. It must have been awful for you. How did you actually come across *the body?*' This time he ostentatiously mouthed the words as though that made a difference.

'I really don't think this is the time for this conversation, dear,' Becky interrupted. Her reluctance at discussing the incident must have been tenfold that of Eleanor's. She seemed to have got over her initial shock, though her face was still pale.

A bell rang, and the children rose together from their different activities scattered around the room, like a flock of birds rising out of a newly planted field, though with much less grace. They ran in circles, screaming. Will's demeanour changed from the friendly Head to I'm-in-charge-here-and-there'll-be-none-of-that. He strode off towards the centre of the room. Bellowing at the children for order and silence.

'I'm sorry,' Eleanor said quietly to Becky after he left. 'If it's too hard for you, then I won't come back. The last thing I wanted to do was to upset anyone.' It was a gamble offering to not return, but she had a feeling it would pay off.

'No, it's fine,' Becky replied. 'It was a shock when we heard she had been found buri — had been found. We were all so certain she had run away with her boyfriend, so you can imagine... It's awful to think that all this time she's been...'

Becky's eyes were full of tears. Her hands clenched. Their close relationship was clear. Working together every day, depending on each other for support, both physically and mentally. Eleanor placed her hand on Becky's clenched grasp. There was no need for words. A quiet smile between them.

The children now sat quietly on the floor. Will returned with a smug look. Proud to have brought the class under control. Becky turned back to the children, and they sat up attentively at her voice.

Will continued talking, though Eleanor hardly listened as they left the classroom, preoccupied with her own lack of tact. She couldn't believe she had given no thought to how her presence would affect others. The memories that it would invoke. Once they reached the staff-room, they sat, each with a coffee, at a circular garden table, just outside the open double doors, while Will jabbered on.

'Nineteen years ago I started here. Came in as the head and shook the place up. And, let me tell you, it needed it. Since then I've taken the school from strength to strength. The classes were nothing more than the minimal number of mixed year groups and now, as you can see, we're at the point of needing to extend.'

One of the back legs of Eleanor's chair suddenly slipped off the edge of the patio and onto the grass. It was only a centimetre drop, but enough to make Eleanor jolt, and a splash of her coffee spilt onto her blouse.

'Oh,' Will exclaimed, with much more exuberance than was necessary. 'Are you alright?'

Eleanor was shaken, but unharmed. 'Yes, yes. I'm fine. I...' she felt her blouse where the coffee had splashed.

'Let me get you some tissues.'

Will disappeared into the staff-room while Eleanor clambered up from the uneven chair and placed her mug on the table. Will returned with a handful of tissues and Eleanor dabbed herself down. Thankfully, she had chosen a patterned blouse that, to some extent, disguised the small coffee stain.

'I guess I had better extend the patio while I'm about extending the school.' His laugh boomed. 'It was new when I arrived and I can remember thinking at the time that I would have laid a much larger patio. Such a shame they laid it without knowing how successful the school was going to become. Unfortunately, some people just don't have the vision needed for this job.'

His self-congratulatory attitude grated on Eleanor's nerves.

'Well, what do you think, Eleanor? If we promise not to throw coffee over you again, are you still willing to join our team?'

'It's a lovely school,' she said. 'I would be thrilled to come and help wherever I can.'

'And what about you? Planning to have any children of your own anytime soon?'

At that moment, the staff-room door opened, and voices drifted through.

'Is it lunchtime already?' She jumped up, quick to avoid the question, or rather, the answer. 'You'll have your checks to do, obviously, but I'm happy to start Monday.'

'I'm sure there won't be any problems. I look forward to seeing you this evening for dinner. It can be a kind of extended interview. And I look forward to meeting your husband too, of course.'

Eleanor thought about trying to explain that Darryl was not her husband, but was interrupted as soon as she opened her mouth.

'Mr Cowley,' a voice called from the staff-room door. 'May we see you for a moment? I'm afraid Simon here has some explaining to do.'

One of the teachers stood at the entrance to the staff-room, a boy of around six or seven years old by her side. The head cocked to one side and eyes down pose was one Eleanor had seen many times with her son, Chris, when he knew he had done something naughty. Times when she had scolded him. Now she longed to put her arms around him and tell him she loved him. Tell him that everything would be alright.

Will jolted her from her thoughts with a cheerful, 'We'll see you at seven, then. We live in the headteacher's house just next door. We can continue your interview then.' He shook her hand and made his way across the staff-room. 'Simon, Simon, Simon. What have you been up to now?'

Eleanor hurriedly finished her coffee, trying to hide her trembling hands. Luckily, the secretary was busy on the phone when she returned to the reception to collect her bag, which meant Eleanor didn't feel like she had to question her. Besides, there would be plenty of time for that during the next couple of weeks. She grabbed her bag and left with a polite smile, relieved to have the chance to escape. She marched from the school and returned to the bench she had sat on before she'd entered. With knees that didn't feel as though they were attached to her legs, she didn't think she could cope with the walk home. Not yet anyway. She sat and stared at the school, taking in everything that had happened that morning. She hoped Darryl wouldn't mind the dinner invitation, but she didn't feel she could have refused. But surely, he would not argue at having the opportunity to question Miss Starling's assistant. She only hoped he took it easy on Becky and didn't become too enthused with his interrogation.

A sense of pride filled her. She had done it. For Miss Starling's sake, she had fought back her own memories and won.

Taking in a deep breath, she smelt the fresh countryside around her. The warm air filling her lungs. Her legs stronger, she rose from the bench, giving a little skip as she walked across the grass towards home. She quickly checked around her as her cheeks flushed. Once she reached the edge of the village, the fields opened out, and Eleanor could see the bus approaching from a couple of miles away. She had just enough time to give Darryl a quick call before it arrived, fancying the idea of going into town. She deserved a treat, and they had several clothes shops there that she hadn't had a chance to go in to yet.

~

Darryl's nerves had been getting the better of him all morning. With all the problems in the house, and then discovering a dead body, he had thought Eleanor close to breaking point. Then came the noises upstairs; someone was breaking into their home. He was almost waiting for the words, "That's it, I've had enough." He could hear her saying them in his head. Instead, something had made her more determined, and she had rallied. After her initial reaction to working at the school, she was up early and eager to get there. There was no sign of her wanting to walk out now. For that, at least, he was grateful.

Once he had left home that morning, he'd found it difficult to focus. At work, the mosaic he had been working on seemed an unending task. He had welcomed the opportunity to excavate a previously unknown Roman mosaic. The first to uncover, to see, to touch the tiles, diligently laid hundreds of years earlier. Already eight feet square and no sign of an edge. Usually, this would excite him. But today it was exhaustive. No matter how much he cleared, there was frustratingly more to uncover. Visitors to the site annoyed him. They ambled past, constantly asking questions and interrupting his thoughts. The earth walls that usually comforted him and gave some shelter from the wind felt oppressive.

Just after half twelve, his phone rang. His hand, filthy from scraping at the dirt, reached into his pocket. Both hesitant and excited to answer.

'I'm in,' were Eleanor's first words.

He laughed with relief, not realising how much he had wanted her to do this. It had worried him she may have changed her mind and was now regretting it, but she was still intent on investigating.

'I hope you don't mind though, the Head and his wife, who just happens to have been Miss Starling's TA at the time of her disappearance,' she added with an air of nonchalance, 'have invited us for dinner tonight.'

'Tonight? Wow, you do work fast. What time?' he asked.

'Seven. Would you be able to get off early?'

'What for?' he asked, wiping the dirt off his hand onto his jeans.

'To give you some time to wash and brush up. You're a mess when you get home.'

'I'm not that bad.' Darryl only heard silence on the phone. 'Am I?'

'Let's just say you're going to at least need a shower.'

'OK, I'll give you that. I'll see you later,' he said. 'Oh, and by the way, congratulations.'

Her thanks told him she knew he wasn't just congratulating her for getting any old job. It would have taken a lot for her to have even set foot through the door of the school, let alone be positive and friendly. She must have done well. *But then again*, he thought mischievously, *Stuck-up Stella had said they were desperate.* He hung up and immediately his phone rang again. It was Rachel. He ignored it and went for his lunch.

During the afternoon, for some reason, the tourists were much more pleasant, and Darryl was only too happy to discuss their work. He and Larry spent the quieter periods reminiscing about their time together uncovering a World War Two bomber several years earlier. Not Darryl's particular interest, but it was a job and turned out to be more fascinating than he had expected. He and Larry had got on well together during the dig and it had been Larry that had put Darryl on to this job at Minstrel-wood after keeping in touch over the years. A Christmas card every year kind of keeping in touch.

Around three o'clock, Darryl's phone rang again. The sight of Rachel's name annoyed him. Why wouldn't she just leave a message? He pressed the decline button and replaced the phone in his pocket.

'I had a feeling you were ignoring me,' came a familiar voice.

Darryl looked up towards a group of visitors who were strolling past, only showing a modicum of interest in the mosaic. The group kept walking, following the visitor barriers that stretched between the path and the mosaic trench, and on towards the next exhibit, a ruined bath house on the other side of the field. One person stayed behind, looking down at him. Rachel.

7

Darryl hung his head. Rachel always had a touch for the dramatic. She stood in her figure-hugging, flowery dress and high-heeled shoes. Just the right attire for traipsing around an archaeological site.

'Couldn't you have just left a message like normal people do?' he asked.

'I need to talk to you and if you're not going to answer your phone you don't give me much option.' She stood looking down at him with her arms folded in a defensive manner.

'So, what's so important?' Grateful for the lull in visitors, Darryl spoke with the disdain he felt.

'Alex,' she replied.

'She's OK, isn't she?' A sudden rush of guilt entered his chest. Maybe he should have answered Rachel's calls.

'Yes, she's fine. If dropping out of university is considered fine.'

'What?' he exclaimed.

'Er, Darryl?' Larry interrupted. 'Do you need to go? I can cover for you the rest of the day.'

'Larry, you're a mate. Thanks.' Darryl turned his attention

back to Rachel. 'I'll meet you at the entrance. I need to get cleaned up.'

∼

Eleanor had decided after her morning at the school that a new dress was called for. Something nice for the dinner that evening. There wouldn't be much time before she would need to get the bus for the hour-long return journey, and so, to save time, she bought a sandwich to eat while she window shopped before entering the clothes shops she favoured.

Today, everything seemed to go her way. Some days, she could hunt and find nothing she liked. Today she knew the dress as soon as she saw it. Simple, yet elegant. Deep green with a subtle low cowl neckline at the back. The tapered waist emerged into a full skirt. Revelling in the flow and swing of the material, she paraded along the short corridor that ran outside the cubicles of the changing rooms. A special feeling would arise when wearing something so beautiful. Something not possible to put into words, nor explain how it changed her demeanour, her posture. It even made her like herself.

She popped into an off-licence on the way back to the bus station to pick up a bottle of wine for the meal.

'Eleanor,' she heard as she exited the shop.

Tourists buffeted their way past her. Finding anyone in the narrow street was near impossible, but she was sure she had heard someone call her. Two-way traffic trundled along the road built with horses and carts in mind, and the pavements on either side were only just wide enough for two abreast. It was a sudden arrival when Stella appeared behind a couple with a pushchair.

'Oh, Eleanor. Carl told me of all the goings on at your house last night. Are you alright?' Stella held on to Eleanor's arm as though worried she would collapse from fright.

'I'm fine, yes,' Eleanor answered, but Stella clearly believed what she had to say was of much more importance and, unaware of the people struggling to get past without needing to step off the curb and into the busy road, she continued.

'But if you will move into a haunted house, I guess you only have yourselves to blame.'

'It wasn't a ghost,' Eleanor said, determined to be heard. 'Not unless ghosts carry torches these days.'

'Well, yes,' Stella said thoughtfully. 'I see what you mean. Although Carl did say that he couldn't catch it and Carl - is - fast. He even said himself it was as though it had vanished into thin air.'

Eleanor smiled apologetically at passers-by, squeezing their way around the two women, while tolerating Stella's ruminations.

'Maybe it was the light of the moon lighting up its corporeal being.' Stella beamed at the thought. 'You have to think of all possibilities. My husband has taught me that.'

'There was no moon,' Eleanor replied bluntly. 'It was cloudy last night. Pitch. Black.'

'Oh,' Stella shrieked suddenly, jolted by a passer-by. 'Oh dear, we seem to be in the way. There's a lovely tea-room here. Shall we pop in? We can have a proper chat, get better acquainted.'

Stella hitched her handbag further onto her shoulder and took a couple of steps in the direction of the tea-room, double backing the way she had come, as though the movement would drag Eleanor down the street. An imaginary thread tied between them. The tea-room, only a few shops along from them, was the same one Eleanor had been in yesterday and the thought of going in there again didn't enthral her.

'I can't. I have a busy evening ahead and need to get the bus home.'

'Oh, that's right. You're going to dinner with Becky and Will tonight, aren't you?'

'How do you know that?' Eleanor asked, startled.

'There goes my big mouth again. One day, it's going to get me into so much trouble. I spoke with Becky earlier. They're looking into buying a new house and nothing much happens in Bramblemere that I don't know about. Come on,' Stella implored, moving closer to the tea-room. 'I'll give you a lift home. You don't want to waste your time sitting on a dusty old bus. I only came into town to see Carl and he's gone back to work, and I don't have another client until this evening. I'm gasping for a coffee. Come on.'

Stella was clearly determined. Eleanor reluctantly agreed, unable to think of any more excuses.

∽

Darryl arranged for Rachel to follow him driving into town. He didn't want to take her home. Eleanor's first meeting with her shouldn't be like this, sprung upon her as a surprise. Instead, he took Rachel to a small tea-room on the main street in the oldest part of town that he had noticed yesterday on his trip to the jewellers.

'Let's make this quick,' he said after ordering their drinks. He remained civil to the best of his abilities, but the feeling of betrayal always lingered whenever he had thought about, let alone seen Rachel.

'Alex won't talk to me. I have no idea why she's dropping out, and I was hoping you could try and get through to her. That's it. That's all I wanted to say. Admit it, it is important.'

'Hasn't she given you any clue?'

Rachel shook her head and thanked the woman who delivered her tea.

'What does Kathy say?' Darryl asked.

'When does Kathy ever say anything? Even if she knows anything, she won't break Alex's confidence. And personally, I don't think it's fair to make her.'

'Don't think it's fair?' Darryl was struggling with Rachel's composure. 'It's not like we're asking who was sticking their fingers in the cake icing. You said it yourself, this is kind of important.'

Rachel tried to hold back a laugh. 'It didn't take long till we found out it was Alex.'

'I'm not here to reminisce.' Darryl stared at her across the top of his coffee mug. Gripping it with both hands.

'You brought it up.'

'Only as an example,' he said through gritted teeth. He stopped and took a deep breath. Avoiding her eyes, he focused on his coffee.

'It's good to see you, Darryl,' Rachel said after a moment's silence. 'I see you're still having trouble getting the dirt out from around your nails.'

Darryl set down his mug and self-consciously hid his hands underneath the table. She always did have a thing about the dirt round his nails. In the early days, he had scrubbed his hands hard, but as time went on, the dirt became embedded until he had to give in to the fact that it was just part of the job.

'This Eleanor must be pretty special,' she went on. 'A permanent position, no moving around from place to place all over the country. It's a shame you couldn't have done the same for me.'

'There it is. You had to get in a little dig. Are we really going to go through this again?'

'I'm just saying things could have worked out differently if you weren't leav—'

'I had to work. I had a family to support, remember?' Darryl stopped abruptly as an awful thought came to him. 'Is this it? Is this why Alex is dropping out of Uni?'

Rachel stared back at him curiously. 'I don't understand,' she said.

'She's pregnant.' Darryl hadn't meant for it to sound like a statement of fact, but that's how it came out.

Rachel seemed to stop breathing. Her face had turned white. After a moment, she released a large breath and growled at Darryl, 'Oh my God, you have to talk to her. Make her see there are other options to dropping out.'

'I'll try, but she was never very good at picking up my calls.'

'I wonder who she gets that from,' Rachel said with sarcasm.

'Do you know where she is now?' Darryl continued, choosing to ignore Rachel's remark.

'No. I think I've persuaded her to finish the year out, but I haven't spoken to her since. She's staying with a friend, but who? I don't know.'

'Male or female friend?' Darryl asked.

'I think we can take a well-educated guess, but I don't know.'

'Do you think it's someone from the university?' Darryl saw the look from Rachel. 'I know, you don't know.'

'Alex sent me some photos from when they were away on their trip.' Rachel hurriedly got her phone from her bag. 'There seemed to be an enormous group of them. Maybe he's in there. You know, someone who looks a little closer than just a friend.'

She searched for the photographs on her phone, her long painted nails clicking on the screen as she tapped and swiped. Darryl pulled his chair round in order to see the screen more clearly.

'Why didn't she send these to me?' he said after the first couple of photographs. 'Looks like they had a great time.'

Rachel had been right. It was a large group of people, at least twenty in one of the group shots. Zip wiring, obstacle courses, sitting round a campfire toasting marshmallows. Everything you would expect from an organised adventure holiday.

It didn't take long before they were both laughing together at their two girls. Alex dancing round the campfire and several selfies with different backdrops, most of them beautiful. Surrounded by forests, hills, and caves. Pictures of Kathy, on the other hand, were sparse. The main one was of her walking out of a lake, fully clothed and looking as though she hadn't enjoyed a swim by choice. Darryl had become amused by Rachel's need to point the girls out, as though he wouldn't be able to recognise his own daughters. He understood now, though, why she had pointed out Kathy in the background of the previous photo. She had been sitting quietly on a large rock beside the lake. It took little imagination to work out what had happened between the two photographs.

The girls were identical to look at, but they had shown very different personalities from a young age. Kathy liked quiet. She was as introverted as Alex was extroverted. A love of people around her, and always on the go.

It didn't take long for Darryl and Rachel to forget about the others in the photographs. They had forgotten they were looking for a possible suspect. They had become absorbed in their own space as they laughed together at their two daughters, grown up and having fun.

~

'After you,' Stella said, presenting the door to Eleanor.

Eleanor looked at the time on her phone and wondered how long she could politely endure Stella's company before asking to leave for home. Stepping up to the tea-room door, she suddenly found she couldn't move. Darryl was sitting at the back of the tea-room. A beautiful black-haired woman sat in the corner with him. Their chairs drawn together, the woman was showing Darryl something on her phone. His face was alive with laughter. And she... she was beautiful.

Stella must have seen him, too. 'Isn't that — it is, isn't it? Who's that with him?' she said curiously.

'I don't know,' Eleanor whispered in reply.

Maybe this was the reason he hadn't mentioned anything about a ring. Maybe it wasn't a ring. Or, more to the point, maybe it wasn't for her. After Eleanor's feeling of being 'not too shabby' in her new dress, she now felt perfectly inadequate.

8

'Well, that says it all, doesn't it?' Stella said with a sad sigh. 'I'm sorry to say, men like that are all the same. They like to sow their seeds wide, so to speak.'

She laughed at her musings, though Eleanor stood numb, staring through the window of the tea-room. Watching Darryl's face light up with each new screen on this beautiful woman's phone. Smiling and laughing, absorbed in the moment.

'And, let's face it,' Stella continued, 'a man like that won't find it too difficult to stray to more than one field.'

Eleanor turned and stared at her in disgust. Darryl wasn't like that, was he?

'Oh, don't get me wrong, but when that other field is...' she turned to look at the woman sat with Darryl, her full-bodied, black hair framing her flawless face, 'full of golden corn and deep red poppies, compared with,' she looked back at Eleanor, 'an allotment?'

Eleanor couldn't speak. A sharp intake of breath was the most she could manage.

'I mean, allotments have their place, but...' Stella made no attempt at tact.

Eleanor backed away from the tea-room, oblivious to the knocks and bumps as she stumbled into people walking past.

'Come on,' Stella said, taking her arm. 'I'll take you home now. Anyway, we can have a chat in the car instead.'

There wasn't much of a conversation in the car on the way home. Plenty of talking, but no conversation. Stella rambled on, mostly about how desirable their cottage was, and that she and Carl had even planned to buy it themselves. *If only you had,* Eleanor wished. *Then it wouldn't have been us in this position.* Most of the time, Eleanor's thoughts took over, but Stella's voice was always there. A constant buzz in the background, like the hum of an electricity pylon. Continuing on without pausing for a reply, for which Eleanor was, for once, grateful.

She couldn't get the image of Darryl and this stranger out of her head. The woman's beauty appalled her. If that's what Darryl wanted, she could never compete. But what pulled her focus more was how happy Darryl looked. The full physical laughter she had witnessed at the tea-room was not something that happened often, especially with the stress of the house and all that came with it. He was relaxed. His face was alive with his broad smile. Whatever this woman had to say to him, he was clearly happy to hear it.

Just over half an hour later, Stella dropped Eleanor off at home. She didn't invite Stella in, nor did Stella enquire. Was it too much to hope for that maybe Stella was capable of a little tact? Eleanor threw the shopping on to her bed, along with her handbag, and sat in the lounge, dazed and quiet. The same thoughts rolling round and round in a continuous cycle, always concluding with the thought, *more secrets.*

∼

His time with Rachel had surprised Darryl. He found he could finally relax in her company. Since he had first discovered about her affairs, he dealt with a constant underlying feeling of mistrust. After the divorce, he had never intended to see her again unless the situation was unavoidable. Now, he was almost grateful to her for turning up at work. He thought he had moved on and put it all behind him, but he had still held on to a lot of tension. That tension was now fading. They had both moved on with their lives. He could never forgive her for what she did, but at least they may be able to be friends, or at least civil, for their kids' sakes.

'Would it be so bad if she *was* pregnant?' Darryl asked quietly. Reminiscing hadn't been so bad, after all.

'At the expense of her education? At least we managed to hold off till my final year,' Rachel said, exasperated.

'Lot of good it did you though, then you were changing nappies and bringing up the girls. What use did you ever make of your degree?'

'That's not the point, Darryl.' Rachel stared at him for a moment before she stood forcefully and left for the bathroom.

Darryl, his shoulders hunched as he leaned on the table, finished his coffee in one last gulp. The tension he thought he had lost poured back in a single moment.

Originally drawn to the tea-room by its architecture and history, Darryl's annoyance spilt over into his surroundings. Framed photographs almost covered the walls, distracting the eye from the building's authentic character. The beams with their carpenter's marks were still prominent after hundreds of years; the bread oven set into the wall with the surrounding brickwork still black from soot. Taking the opportunity of a quiet moment to look around, the photographs still pulled his focus. Especially once he recognised the scenes of Bramblemere. On closer inspection, he recognised many of the scenes around the room. Not only Bramblemere, but of other surrounding areas, too. One of the photographs near him was a group of school children outside the primary school at Bramblemere. Knowing how valuable photographic evidence can be for archaeological investigations, he wondered about the children. The date in the bottom left corner of the photograph was twenty years ago. If that photograph was taken twenty years ago, then maybe some of the others were too. About to inspect further, Rachel returned to the table.

'It's time for me to get back,' she said, standing behind her seat. 'Didn't you say you had a dinner engagement you needed to get back for?'

Darryl checked his watch; it was almost six o'clock. They had been a lot longer than he had expected.

'Shit. I've gotta run,' he said, pulling his jacket up over his shoulders. 'I'll be in touch if I find out anything.'

'No,' Rachel called after him. 'Just be in touch.'

He hesitated at the door before he turned and left. He needed to hurry to make it in time for the dinner. He tried to call Eleanor's mobile as he rushed to the car, but all he got was the answerphone.

~

Eleanor's relief at hearing the car pull into the driveway did little to settle her nerves. Her relief was far outweighed by her anger. Seeing Darryl with another woman had been hard enough, but now he was nearly an hour late home. Fifty minutes, or thereabouts. Another fifty minutes for that moment to play over and over in her mind. Each time, the images grew more vivid. Darryl's laugh more exaggerated. The swish of the woman's hair as she flicked it back from her face, more flamboyant.

Wondering what he had been doing in those extra fifty minutes, the words of Stella churned through her mind.

"Men like that..." What kind of man was Darryl? Did she really know him at all? Why was he with this woman, especially when he was supposed to be at work? All afternoon she had longed to know the answers to these questions, but also, she was afraid to.

Arguments in her head hadn't stopped since she'd got home. One moment sitting upright and tense on a kitchen chair, then the next, pacing the length of the kitchen. Now he was here, she didn't want to speak to him at all.

'I'm sorry I'm late, but you'll never guess what happened at work today,' he said, rushing in through the back door.

'I don't want to hear it.' Eleanor said, infuriated by his cheery tone. She knew that the important thing that had happened to him today didn't happen at work.

'But—'

'We don't have time. Go have your shower. You need it after playing in the dirt all day,' she said, almost spitefully.

Darryl hesitated, but then left the room. She thought she heard him mumble something under his breath, but she ignored it.

Eleanor listened to the sound of his footsteps as he jogged up the stairs before she risked venturing out into the hallway. As soon as he was in the bathroom, she ran into the bedroom to get changed herself. Throwing on the dress she had bought that day, she stood and looked at herself in the mirror. Red faced and saggy. Even old. She endeavoured to remember the feeling she'd had in the shop when she had tried it on. Forcing a smile, she pushed her shoulders back and stood tall. Forcing her posture to where it should be, where it had been when it had come so naturally in the shop's dressing room. She had felt so good. But looking at herself now, she felt inept. She felt like... like an allotment.

The hum of the shower stopped, and she quickly pulled off the dress. *I'll return it next week,* she thought as she returned the dress to its bag and threw it into the back of the wardrobe. She grabbed one of her old dresses and yanked it on over her head. Clutching at her handbag and the bottle of wine she had bought that afternoon; she ran back to the lounge, her buttons down the front of her dress still undone in her rush. Halfway down the hallway, the creaking floorboards from Darryl's footsteps began the descent down the stairs.

'How long have we got?' he called down to her.

'Ten minutes,' she replied.

She wished she hadn't spent so much time pacing this afternoon. She could have spent that time preparing for this evening. It may be possible for Darryl to get ready in ten minutes. Men do. But so much more is expected of a woman. The best Eleanor could hope for was clean clothes and a bit of make-up thrown on. As it was, everything felt as though it had a film of dust in this house, even when clean out of the washing. Ten minutes later Darryl strolled into the lounge looking immaculate. Eleanor was hassled and her face flushed.

Darryl came over to her and held her. 'There's no need to worry,' he said. 'You've already done the hard part. You got the job.'

She could hardly bring herself to look at him, to see him smiling back at her. She felt sick. Eleanor wondered if the woman had liked her present. What would he have bought her? A bracelet? Earrings?

'We've got to go,' she said bluntly, and pulled herself away.

9

Eleanor's sharp tone was more than enough proof for Darryl to see she was struggling with her emotions. Her determination to see this through was admirable, but at what cost? Not taking her abruptness personally was difficult, but Darryl remained silent while she provided names and basic details during the ten-minute journey to the schoolhouse. He had hoped to tell her about the old photographs he had seen in the tea-room, but he hadn't had the chance to tell her about Rachel yet, so that was going to have to wait. He didn't want to cloud her head with any more worries than was necessary.

Will and Becky welcomed them at the door with smiles, handshakes, and feigned surprise for the wine. A noisy outburst from the back of the house broke the polite introductions.

'Sorry about that,' said Becky. 'A friend is here and playing with the kids.'

'You probably know him,' Will added, inspecting the bottle of wine, though only briefly. His furrowed brow gave the notion it did not impress him. 'He's the local detective chief inspector. Your paths have probably crossed, what with *the discovery*.'

His pompous laugh took Darryl by surprise and second thoughts crept in whether this was such a good idea.

'We had a quick meeting this afternoon,' Will continued. 'He always takes school security very seriously and is extremely keen to create good relationships between the children and figures of authority. Get them while they're young, that's what I say.'

A door at the end of the hall opened, and DCI Hanson emerged. Two children were pulling on his jacket sleeves, trying to drag him back. A girl of around six years of age sliding along the tiled floor in her socks, dragged by the DCI, brought back memories of Darryl's own girls when they were that age. They had pretended to be holding on to him to stop him from leaving for work. But he had believed it was more of a case that they enjoyed sliding across the floor.

The older child, a boy of around nine, was having a little more success at pulling him back, but ultimately the DCI was too strong.

'Just one more. You don't have to go yet,' the boy implored.

The girl giggled manically, enjoying their game of tug of war.

'Come on, you two,' Becky said as she went to rescue the DCI. 'Come and meet some new neighbours.'

The two children gave up their game and sulked their way down the hall. Already dressed in their pyjamas and dressing gowns, they stood next to their father and politely said hello.

'Hi,' Darryl replied, but Eleanor crouched in front of them.

'I'm Eleanor, and this is Darryl. What are your names?'

'Tommy,' the older child said. 'You were at the school today.'

'That's right. Were you there?' Eleanor asked. 'Nobody introduced us.'

'I was very busy,' Tommy replied, importantly.

'Then it's a good job we weren't, Tommy. I wouldn't have

wanted to disturb you. It's nice to meet you.' Eleanor shook his hand and turned to the younger child.

The girl looked at the floor, her cheeks flushed.

'Come on, Lizzie, tell her your name,' said Tommy.

After a moment's pause, it was clear Lizzie's shyness was too strong. Instead, Eleanor continued, 'Lizzie? Is that your name?'

The girl nodded, still staring at the floor.

'Well, it's very nice to meet you both.'

'Time for bed, now,' Will told them, clapping his hands loudly, causing everyone to jump.

'But we want to play with Uncle Carl.' Lizzie frowned.

'The children have already eaten,' Will said, ignoring Lizzie's protest. Even though he was speaking to Darryl and Eleanor, he could not turn off his authoritative tone.

'And now,' Becky said, crouching and putting an arm around each child, 'it's time for you to go off to bed. Go on.'

'And they have strict instructions to keep to their rooms,' Will boomed as they ambled their way to the stairs.

'I think it's only fitting to introduce myself as Carl.' The DCI interrupted the family commotion. 'This is a social occasion, after all. We didn't exactly meet under the best of circumstances, but I hope you won't hold it against me.'

'Of course not,' Eleanor replied.

Darryl tried to focus on Carl, but the conversation between Becky and her children distracted him.

'Now, no interruptions,' she whispered. 'You know Daddy doesn't like it.' She kissed each one on the forehead. 'Off you go and I'll be up later to tuck you in.'

'I'll be going now, then, Will,' said Carl. 'I don't want to interrupt your evening. Thanks for the update and I'll schedule in next Tuesday for the assembly.' Carl gave a cheery nod to everyone and left.

Will led Eleanor into the lounge, while Darryl fell behind,

watching Becky. She stood at the bottom of the stairs and watched her children longingly as they dragged themselves off to bed.

Daddy doesn't like interruptions, Darryl thought, *but Mummy would be more than happy to have them with her downstairs.*

On entering the lounge, Darryl felt like he had stepped back in time, and not in a good way. Two lamps were the only light in the dark room. A standard lamp in the far corner and a table lamp beside the drinks cabinet. The brown shades, along with similar decor in the room, gave a distinct 1960s feel. Which in itself wasn't a bad thing, only that the overall feel was gloomy and depressing.

'I know you teachers only too well,' Will was saying to Eleanor. 'Not able to switch off that nurturing instinct. I would say that comes with the job, but no, I believe the job comes because of the instinct.'

Will's self-pride in his attempt at a philosophical observation amused Darryl, and he tried to hide his smile, turning his attention to a family portrait on the wall as a distraction.

'Drink anyone?' Becky asked as she entered the room and offered from an extensive selection.

Eleanor had briefly explained in the car that Becky was having a hard time with her friend's body being found. Even so, she poured drinks with a smile and bestowed compliments for Eleanor's dress. *The perfect hostess*, Darryl thought. Eleanor, taking a large glass of red wine, looked calm and as though she belonged. He was sure he could sense an affinity between them.

Well done, Eleanor, he thought, *I think you've missed your calling.* His only regret was that he didn't get to tell her about Rachel. But then, the mood she had been in, it probably wouldn't have been a good time, anyway. For the next half an hour, Becky popped in and out to the kitchen to deal with the final preparations for the dinner, allowing her husband to stay and talk. And talk. The conversation was polite, even if dull. Already knowing a little about Eleanor, Will turned his attention to Darryl.

'An archaeologist! I have always found archaeology fascinating.' He took a large gulp of his wine. 'It was one of the reasons I moved to this area. To be immersed in so much history. Did you hear that, love?' Will called to Becky as she walked through the door, returning from the kitchen. 'He's an archaeologist at the Minstrel-Wood site.' Turning his attention back to Darryl, he continued, 'The number of times I have arranged for the children to visit that site is endless. For nearly twenty years, I've managed to wrangle it for one class or another to go along.' He downed the rest of his glass. 'And, as Becky can't drive, it always comes down to me to drive the minibus. So, of course, I have to join them on the tour.' His round face beamed as he helped himself to a second glass of wine. 'I'll look out for you next time. Maybe you can give us all a guided tour from an insider's point of view.'

Darryl fixed his smile. He nodded gently, but couldn't bring himself to say anything. Instead, he changed the subject.

'And what about you, Will? Where were you before you graced Bramblemere with your presence?' He avoided Eleanor's stare.

'Ahh,' Will sighed, oblivious to Darryl's sarcasm. 'I spent a couple of years in a four-form entry, but it was too much. Obviously, I could cope with it,' he added with a gentle laugh, 'but it wasn't what I wanted. I found it didn't have the community feel I strive for. But as you can probably imagine with 120 new children entering the school every year, it's not easy. I like everybody working together, pulling together for a common goal and that's difficult to achieve in such a large school. In fact, I would go so far as to say it's impossible.'

Because you couldn't, Darryl thought, but remained silent.

'And now,' Will went on, 'after being here for nearly twenty years, I see those earlier children as adults, and it gives me tremendous pleasure to see them as the great, well-respected members of the community they are. It gives me a sense of pride to know that I was even just a small part of their journey.'

Darryl's focus had wandered. Trying his best to look interested in Will's conversation, he couldn't help but notice Eleanor's gaze had followed Becky out of the room. It looked as though she was about to follow her when Becky returned and announced that dinner was ready.

Will led Darryl and Eleanor through to the dining room. On entering, Darryl seated himself on the farther side of the centrally placed square table.

'You'll have to forgive the cosiness of the room,' Will said jovially. 'They did not build these old headmaster houses for large numbers.' He pulled out a chair for Eleanor. 'Or even small numbers if it comes to it.'

He opened another bottle of wine and offered to both Eleanor and Darryl. After their refusal for more, he topped up his own glass.

'We have been thinking of turning the house into offices for the school. Classroom sizes are growing, thanks to my guidance, and this house would work well as offices, or perhaps an extended classroom. We, ourselves, could do with somewhere a little bigger, too. Especially now our own children are growing, we won't all fit soon.'

All three were now seated, and it soon became apparent that, so long as the chairs remained tucked under, there was room to move. But now, if Darryl wanted to leave the table, there was no escape without disturbing someone. The same darkness furnished the dining room as did the lounge. Even the central mock chandelier that hung above the table seemed to be set to dim. He could understand their need for more space.

'Discussions were even had about having a look at your place before you came along and snapped it up,' Will continued as Becky brought through two of the meals. 'Though Becky wasn't so keen, were you, love?'

Becky simply shook her head and left to get the other two plates, leaving her husband to carry on.

'Too big, she says. As if there is such a thing. Although I'd imagine there are a few rooms to spare, especially with just the two of you.'

'Lots of rooms, yes,' said Eleanor, 'but only a couple in a usable condition. We're even having to use the dining room as our bedroom at the moment. I'm afraid we have a lot of work to do before we'll be able to return the invitation.'

'Plenty of time for that. Get yourselves sorted first.' Will relaxed into his chair, raising his glass. 'Then you'll have yourselves a lovely *family* home.'

Darryl choked on his wine. 'Wow, you really are keen on enlarging that school,' he said with a nervous laugh.

'Wouldn't you like children? Especially you Eleanor?'

Eleanor went rigid. 'I — I—' she stammered.

Darryl scrambled with his thoughts to take the focus off Eleanor. He was about to announce he had twins, but Will got there first.

'I'm sorry,' Will said, furrowing his brow. Unfortunately, his attempt at sympathy came across as patronising. 'It's obviously something you don't want to talk about. We've had our fair share of problems in that department too, haven't we, dear?' he motioned towards Becky as she returned with the remainder of the meals.

She joined them at the table and simply smiled as a reply, but it was the same sad smile that Darryl had seen from Eleanor many times when they had first met. A smile that only the death of a loved one could produce. From the forlorn look, he knew Eleanor had noticed it too.

Will reached across the table and put a hand on Eleanor's. 'We understand,' he said. 'We'll say no more.' He picked up his knife and fork and continued, the sensitivity of the subject forgotten. 'We had a couple of miscarriages ourselves before our two came along.'

Eleanor, who was still watching Becky, whipped her head round with such a look of disdain on her face Darryl was concerned she was going to say something he knew she would regret.

'In fact, we were even told it would never be possible. And now look. Now, I'm not putting doctors down. They do an amazing job, but our two upstairs just go to prove that Mother Nature can work miracles,' Will continued.

Darryl struggled to change the subject, but the statement had dumbfounded him, too. Luckily, Becky spoke.

'It's very nice of you to come and help at the school.' Becky had spent most of the evening silent and inconspicuous, and even now, her voice was soft and reserved. 'I hope you don't mind being the TA rather than the teacher.'

'I don't mind at all,' Eleanor said. 'I wouldn't be ready to go back to teaching after such a long break.'

'Were you travelling?' Becky asked. 'That seems to be all the rage these days.'

Eleanor faltered.

'Amazing lamb, this,' Darryl interrupted. 'Lamb can be so tricky. This is, dare I say it, perfect.'

'Thank you,' Becky said, turning her eyes towards her lap.

'Amazing cook, my wife. Even went away on a course, didn't you love? Just for my benefit. How's that for devotion?' Will poured himself another glass of wine. He didn't bother offering to anyone else.

'I guess we need to discuss what time you'd like me to start Monday morning,' Eleanor said, focused towards Will.

Darryl squirmed in his seat; her tone had turned. *Keep it together, Eleanor.*

'Why don't we say around eight-thirty?' Will seemed unaware of her strained intonation. 'You can just wander in with the children. I think the best time to see them is at that handover time. They leave their parent as one child and come into school as quite another. Becky does wonders with them in class, but then, Becky does wonders everywhere. Baking cakes for the village fete, organising one event or another. A true wonder.' His devotion to his wife slurred; his cheeks blotched with red.

Darryl had lost count of how many times Will had refilled his glass, but noticed that, like himself, Eleanor's glass was still half full.

'How are you finding life in Bramblemere?' Becky asked quietly.

Darryl had the feeling that she was desperately attempting to move the conversation away from herself.

'It's beautiful here,' Eleanor said. 'And so peaceful.'

'If you don't mind the odd dead body in your garden. A minor hiccup, eh?' Will boomed with a laugh. 'You were good friends with the woman, weren't you, love? Didn't you say?'

'Well, we worked together. I guess you could say we got quite close, probably closer than anyone else in the village.'

'Why do you say that?' asked Eleanor. 'Was she not popular in the village?'

'Nothing like that. She always kept herself to herself. She was great with the kids but seemed to struggle when it came to adults.'

'Except one, I understand,' Darryl said.

Becky looked at him questioningly.

'Her boyfriend?'

'Oh yes, her boyfriend. I never met him, but she never stopped talking about him and how he was going to come and... and...' Becky stumbled over her words, as though trying to remember what she was saying, 'and join her soon. When she... when she disappeared, we all thought they had... they had run off together. I'm sorry — I — I must check on the dessert.' She rushed out of the room.

Will continued eating as though nothing had happened.

'Should I go see if she's alright?' Eleanor asked tentatively.

'No, no, she's fine,' Will said. 'It's best to let her work these things out on her own. You'll see. She'll be back in a moment as though nothing has happened.'

Eleanor stared at Will, open-mouthed.

'It must have been an enormous shock for her when Miss Starling was discovered in our garden after all these years,' Darryl said quickly, before Eleanor had a chance to say anything.

'It hit her hard. There's no denying that,' Will said. 'I think it was a tremendous shock for everyone. They had all convinced themselves of some romantic notion that she and this mysterious boyfriend had walked off into the sunset hand in hand.'

Darryl quietly smirked as Will struggled to pronounce the word mysterious.

'And then this happens.' Will reached across the table for the wine bottle.

'I'm sorry. We didn't mean to upset her,' Eleanor whispered.

Will waved his knife in the air in a don't-worry gesture while he gulped down another large mouthful of his wine.

'Do you know much about the time Miss Starling went missing?' Darryl asked while Eleanor sat back heavily in her chair, resigning herself to the situation.

'No, it happened a few months before I arrived.'

'Are there many people still at the school that would have remembered her?' Darryl politely continued between mouthfuls of his meal.

Will lent back in his chair thoughtfully.

'Susan, the school secretary, has been there forever, but everybody else has moved on. Even Becky was thinking about moving away when I arrived, but I managed to persuade her to stay and train to become a teacher. She's the best we have now.'

'What do you think made her change her mind?' Darryl asked.

'Love,' Will said, and he raised his glass as though making a toast. A line of red ran through his greying beard, leading to a drip, which he wiped with a large sweep of the back of his hand. 'She had just gone through a bad break-up with her boyfriend when I arrived,' Will said, losing control of his spittle. 'He had run out on her and left the village. She wanted to move away and make a new start. Although, she was looking after her mother at the time, who was very ill with MS. She would never... never, ever have moved away from her mother. That was when I first saw her true beauty.' His eyes glazed over as he lovingly remembered the Becky from years ago. 'She cared for her mother relentlessly. Multiple sclerosis is a nasty business, but she never complained or stopped taking care of her mother's every possible want or need. That's when I thought, this is the woman I want to spend the rest of my life with. And so, we fell in love, and I hate to use a cliche, but the rest is... is... what is it?'

'History,' all three said together.

At that moment, Becky walked back into the room. Everyone had finished their meals except Becky, who had hardly touched hers.

'Are we all ready for dessert?' she asked, as though the previous conversation hadn't happened. A smile on her face, but her eyes were red and puffy from crying.

10

'Well, that went well, don't you think?' Eleanor said sarcastically as Darryl drove out of the village and headed for home.

They had left Becky waving from her doorstep while Will was still in his armchair. He had fallen asleep soon after their meal, and Becky seemed only too pleased to keep it that way.

'Don't think we learned anything new, if that's what you mean.' Darryl sighed heavily and listed the conversations like a checklist. 'Becky was Miss Starling's assistant at the time she disappeared. They were obviously close; it wasn't a conversation she relished. And there was a boyfriend, but nobody ever saw him or even knew his name. Anything I've forgotten?'

'The secretary, she was working at the school then, too.' Eleanor said. 'She acted quite strangely this morning, and doesn't seem the type for gossip. I have a feeling she's going to be difficult to get into a conversation.' Eleanor drifted into her own thoughts.

'And the secretary was there too,' Darryl added to his list.

He was tired and didn't want to ask what had happened with the secretary. He was grateful for the quiet that followed. He hadn't even drunk half his glass of wine, but he was glad he hadn't had anymore.

'I was just thinking about Becky's two miscarriages,' Eleanor said after a couple of minutes. 'That must have been awful and such a shame when she does so much for the community and everyone else.'

'It's a pity she doesn't give herself so much consideration,' Darryl mumbled, more to himself than to Eleanor.

'What do you mean?' she asked.

'Well, she does so much for the village and for her husband. The house was spotless. The kids adored her. She's perfect, except...'

'Except?'

Darryl, aware of digging a hole that he might not be able to clamber out of, struggled for the right words. 'She doesn't use any of that care and thoughtfulness for herself.'

'Meaning?'

'She looked... dull.' That was the best word he could think of without being outright rude.

'Dull?'

'Yeah, dull. Her hair, for example, was... dull. Limp and hanging forward, covering her face.'

'Are you judging her by her hair?' Eleanor asked.

'No, I'm just saying—'

'Of all the good things she does for other people, and for the community,' Eleanor interrupted, 'the most important thing to you is how she looks.'

Darryl knew Eleanor well enough by now to know that it was not a good sign when she turned her head away and stared out the side window, quietly seething.

'I'm not judging her. I'm saying that with all the good she does for everyone else, it's a shame she doesn't use some of that good for herself.'

'Because a woman looking beautiful like a... a field of golden corn is the overriding factor of a woman's contribution to the world,' Eleanor snapped.

'What? You know that's not how I think.' He swerved into their driveway and stopped hard.

'Isn't it?'

'No. Look, doesn't it make you feel better when you look good?' Parked on their driveway, Darryl turned to look at her properly, but she avoided his eyes.

Eleanor stared down at her lap. Tugging at the sides of her skirt.

'Doesn't it give you a kind of confidence?' he continued.

'But you don't think we can get that confidence from the things we do? It has to be from how we look?'

'That's not what I'm saying at all. She's clearly not very fond of herself and so doesn't think she should spend time on herself.'

Eleanor gasped and stared disbelievingly at Darryl.

'She's clearly downtrodden by an over-bearing husband who talks more than he listens,' Eleanor said forcefully. 'He doesn't love her; he loves the idea of being married to such a community spirited woman and it reflects well on him. He has no empathy what-so-ever for her feelings. Miss Starling's death clearly upset her and you two just carried on as though it were a pleasant topic of conversation.'

'I don't think that's fair. We did wait till she'd left the room.'

Eleanor got out of the car and slammed the door. The sound reverberated through Darryl's bones. He waited a moment before following her. He was too tired for an argument and purposefully fell behind as he followed her round to the front of the house. Eleanor, striding ahead, had disappeared round the corner before he'd left the car. As he approached the front door, he saw Eleanor bending over something large on the doorstep. Mostly hidden behind her, he couldn't make out what it was until he was much closer. A woman was leaning against the front door, asleep. Her shoulders subconsciously hunched from cold. A well-worn rucksack by her side.

Eleanor had placed her hand on the strange woman's shoulder and was gently shaking her. 'Are you alright? Can I help you?' she asked.

The woman stirred and, embarrassed, she sprung to her feet. She brushed the dirt from her coat where she had sat on the stone flag.

'I'm sorry. I must have fallen asleep,' she said. 'I'm so sorry. What must you think of me?' She gave a short, nervous laugh.

'We might think more of you if we knew who you were,' said Darryl.

'Of course,' the woman said, startled. 'I'm Amelia, Amelia Nightingale.'

The matter-of-fact statement and the silence that followed made Darryl think maybe they should recognise the name, but Eleanor had the same puzzled expression as he did.

'I'm Jenny's sister.'

Again, there was no recognition.

'Jennifer Nightingale. The woman you found in—' She paused. Her eyes darted down towards her feet, unable to finish the sentence.

'Miss Starling?' Eleanor asked.

'Yes, well, no. Her name wasn't Starling. It was Nightingale. Jennifer Nightingale.' She gave another snatch of nervous laughter. 'I'm sorry, I thought you would have been told.'

∼

Eleanor, Darryl and Amelia Nightingale stood in silence on the doorstep. It took a moment before Eleanor pulled herself together.

'Please, come in,' she stammered while the realisation of what this stranger had said sank in.

Amelia's hands trembled as she picked up her rucksack and entered the house, though probably more to do with nerves than the cool evening. After declining a hot drink, Eleanor brought Amelia a blanket. She perched on the edge of the sofa, her pale face looking terrified. Her grey streaked hair, ruffled from sleeping on their doorstep.

'I'm afraid we won't be able to help you,' Eleanor said. 'We know nothing about her or her death. We only moved here three weeks ago.'

'You already have helped me,' Amelia said, her voice quivering. 'I've been searching for her for twenty-six years. I'd almost given up when the police arrived and said they'd found her body. Killed at the hands of her boyfriend, at least that's their theory. But I know, I *know* that's not true. She wouldn't have, *couldn't* have — I'm sorry,' she said, reining herself in. She continued hesitantly, 'I came to - I was hoping I'd be able to see the place where she was...'

Eleanor moved to sit next to Amelia and reached for her hand. 'Of course, we'll help in whatever way we can. I wish we could do more.'

'Why do you think she wasn't killed by her boyfriend?' asked Darryl.

'I know she wasn't,' Amelia said firmly. She pulled her hand away from Eleanor's grasp and squeezed her fingers anxiously as she spoke. 'She was in hiding from her husband. Ian was abusive, both physically and mentally. Her confidence and her nerves were shattered.'

The impact of Ian's abuse went further than his wife, even

after so many years. Amelia sat with her shoulders hunched under the blanket, making balls with her fists; her knuckles white with rage.

'She eventually managed to escape him,' Amelia went on, 'but wouldn't even tell me where she'd gone to protect me. After a couple of years, she sent me a letter to let me know she was building a life for herself, and she was safe.

'Of course, I was overjoyed to hear from her, but Ian was in prison by then and was going to be there a long time. He had got into a fight in a pub and killed a man. Finally, it meant she could come home. But I had no idea where she was or how to contact her. Every few months, I would receive either a postcard or a letter, but always sent from different places. Tracing her was impossible.'

Amelia pulled a batch of postcards and letters from her rucksack. The bundle was around three inches thick and bound carefully with an old, faded lilac ribbon. Darryl took the stack and flicked through them as she continued with her narrative.

'That carried on for a few more years, but then, twenty years ago, they stopped with no warning or explanation.'

'Was Ian still in prison at this point?' Darryl asked.

'He never left. He finally picked a fight with the wrong person and was killed in his cell. I carried on searching for nearly ten years, but then hired a private detective, Connor, Connor Dobson.' She smiled fondly as she said his name. 'I just couldn't do it on my own. Five years ago, he was following a lead, but he didn't want to tell me any more than that. A few times he had thought he was on her track, only to find it was a wild goose chase. He didn't want to get my hopes up again. All I know is, he headed to this county, and that was the last I heard from him.

'When I went to the police about his disappearance, nobody would listen. I was told I'd been duped. He'd taken my money and disappeared. But he wouldn't have done that. Six years we had been working on this together. He was almost as obsessed as I was.' Again, Amelia reined herself in. Gripping tightly to the edges of the blanket. She took a deep intake of air. 'They told me they'd look into it,' she continued, 'but I heard nothing from them. I don't believe they even tried. Until this morning when someone knocked on my door to tell me a body, known as Amelia Starling, had been found. Apparently, she had changed her name by deed poll, so when they found her real name, they came across the missing person's report I had made for Jenny years ago.

'Obviously it's her. I have no doubt that it is. She even changed her name to mine, Amelia.' Tears welled in her eyes, and she pulled the blanket tighter around her shoulders. 'But I don't believe she was killed by a boyfriend,' she said aggressively. 'Ian had left her scarred and terrified. Read the letters and you'll see. She was having trouble relating to anyone, male, female, it made no difference.'

'And so, she changed her name to Starling, and began again. A new name, a new life,' Eleanor said.

'I'm sure you would probably like to forget the whole thing,' Amelia said with an apologetic smile. 'It couldn't have been nice to have...' her voice drifted off.

Eleanor could tell that the image of her dead sister's bones, rising out of the earth, had just emerged into Amelia's head as she fought to continue.

'I tried to tell the police that there was no way she would have had a boyfriend, especially at the time this would have happened. But they just pushed it aside and told me I couldn't have known what was going on in her life as I hadn't seen her for so long. Of course, they tried to put it more diplomatically than that, but that's what it came down to.'

Amelia could no longer hold back her tears and Eleanor knew better than to try to and stop her. Instead, she put her arm around her and let her cry. Darryl, looking awkward, distracted himself by looking through the pile of postcards and letters while Eleanor and Amelia rocked gently on the sofa.

After a few minutes, Amelia pulled herself together. 'I need to go home tomorrow, but I would really like to—' she stammered. 'Would it be possible for me — I was just hoping that I could—'

'You want to see where she's been all this time,' Eleanor said for her.

Amelia nodded, turning her focus to her lap.

'The police won't let me see her body, for obvious reasons, and I certainly wouldn't recognise her, anyway. But I need to see something tangible, something real to prove that all this is actually happening. That she *is* dead.'

'Of course,' Eleanor said. 'The garden is still cordoned off, and it's too dark now to see anything from the back door. Where are you staying?'

'I saw a pub in the village from the taxi and was going to see if they had a room, but I didn't expect to fall asleep on your doorstep. I'm so sorry.'

'It's getting on for one o'clock,' Darryl said, looking at the time on his phone. 'I don't think they'll let you in now, they'll be shut.'

Eleanor pleaded with him with her eyes.

'You can stay here tonight,' he said.

'The house is in a state, I'm afraid,' Eleanor said. 'You take our room, and we'll stay in here.'

'No, don't be silly. I'll be fine on the sofa. I've slept in worse places on my travels to find Jenny, believe me.'

'No, I insist. You've had a long day and you're exhausted. I'll take you and show you where everything is. Darryl, could you…' Eleanor indicated the sofas and Darryl begrudgingly nodded.

Darryl, Eleanor and Amelia prepared themselves for the night. Darryl understood Eleanor's reasoning, nevertheless, giving up his bed had not been his intention. Thankfully, their lounge was large enough to accommodate two decent sized sofas, so there was no arguing over who would have to sleep on the floor. They said no more as they covered themselves in the blankets he had arranged for them and laid down to sleep. Even though their previous *misunderstanding*, as he had convinced himself to think of it, had been interrupted by Amelia's arrival, it had not been forgotten. Eleanor had been on edge all evening. Her nerves would have been in tatters from the anxiety of going back to work in a school; constantly being reminded of her son. It couldn't have been easy for her. *Oh damn*, he thought. *I still haven't told her about Rachel. Haven't exactly had much of a chance though.*

'Eleanor!' he called gently, hoping she was already asleep. Probably not the best conversation for the middle of the night, but he needed to try. He was relieved, though, when she didn't reply. It would have to wait till morning.

～

Eleanor laid quietly. She heard Darryl calling her, but she didn't feel like talking to him. He had mentioned nothing about the woman in the cafe or the trip to the jewellers. What lies would he tell next?

11

Darryl turned restlessly. He arched his back in an effort to stretch out the ache. The creaks of the uncomfortable sofa joined the groans of the floorboards with each move. Maybe sleeping on the floor would be more desirable. Never having the need for a spare room before, his mind wandered to working out how he could organise one of the other bedrooms and bump it up the priority list along with the master bedroom. It was gone three o'clock before he began drifting into sleep. Searching in his dream for the fire, he could smell. He turned uncomfortably again. His heavy eyelids opened sleepily. Was it sleep in his eyes or smoke causing the haze that filled the room?

Waking fully with a jolt, smoke poured into his lungs as he gasped from the shock. Choking, he sat up and saw Eleanor still sleeping peacefully.

'Eleanor, Eleanor,' he called, and leapt across the room to wake her. She stirred slowly at first. 'Fire. There's a fire. Wake up.' The words must have suddenly hit her. Either that or the smoke had reached the back of her throat and she sat up, startled.

'Come on, we've got to get out,' he said as he pulled at her arm.

They stumbled to the lounge door that led into the hallway, smoke drifting in underneath. Darryl hesitated. Dreading what laid behind, while Eleanor double-backed and snatched up their phones from the coffee table. Darryl forced himself to open the door and thick black smoke billowed in. He moved back to let the worst of it clear before stepping out into the hallway. His eyes drawn towards the fire, he saw something on the rug at the foot of the front door. He didn't have time to make out what it was until the flames overwhelmed it. The rug beneath it became nothing more than a rectangle of flames. The smoke had drifted along the hall and, luckily, through the sizeable gaps around the lounge door. Gaps Eleanor had constantly complained about causing draughts. But now, without those gaps, things could have been a lot worse.

The fire hadn't yet reached the boxes that lined the wall of the hallway. Boxes they hadn't yet got around to opening since they moved in, but Darryl knew it wouldn't be long before they too were engulfed in flames.

'Call the fire brigade,' he said, pushing Eleanor towards the kitchen at the back of the house and away from the fire. 'I'll get Amelia.'

Eleanor left, keeping low as she rushed to get out. Darryl followed her along the hallway towards the door for their makeshift bedroom. A sudden roar of flames behind him forced him to duck. The stinging heat on his back compelled him to quicken his steps further. A quick glance back showed the flames had taken hold of the thick curtains that hung on either side of the front door. The heat scorched at his face as he turned to the dining-room door. Darryl's nerves surged through him and he burst noisily into the bedroom. The commotion woke Amelia before he reached her.

'We've got to get out,' Darryl called. 'The house is on fire.'

Amelia, stunned, looked around her. Her eyes wide with fear.

'The fire's at the front door,' he continued. 'It won't take long to get along the hall.'

Amelia still looked dazed by her sudden awakening.

'Do you understand?' he asked.

She nodded briefly. 'Fire,' she whispered.

It could have been shock, sleepiness, or terror that had taken her voice, or a combination of all three. But there was no time to find out.

Darryl grabbed a couple of t-shirts from a drawer. Passing one to Amelia, they held them in front of their faces, trying to stop the smoke from entering their lungs.

They dashed across the hallway. Darryl couldn't resist a quick glance as he went. The first couple of boxes and their contents alight. He pushed thoughts of the damage occurring to his beloved home away and focused on keeping everybody safe. He followed Amelia through to the kitchen and closed the door behind him. Eleanor was already outside the back door, talking on the phone to the emergency services and shivering in the cold and dark. Her voice was shrill and deafening in the silence of the night.

Darryl had only had this house for three weeks. For a short three weeks, he had been its custodian, its guardian. He had failed, and his heart ached with helplessness. He heard the fire engine's wail long before it arrived, or so it seemed. The problems of narrow country roads. However long it was, it was too long.

A paramedic car arrived soon after the fire engine and hustled Eleanor and Amelia into the back of a police car with silver foil blankets, warming them from the night air and the shock, and still in their pyjamas. Darryl fought against it to begin with. Not able to tear himself away from the sight of his beloved home. He finally conceded to the blanket, but he watched, standing away from the commotion as the firefighters worked, but never too far. The sun was rising now, and as time passed, he found his legs wouldn't hold him any longer and he joined Eleanor and Amelia in the police car, taking the front seat. Leaning his head against the window, tears ran down his face, not able to take his eyes off the house.

Soon, one of the firefighters came towards the police car. Darryl, eager to hear any news, hurried out of the car.

'Richard Atkins,' he announced. 'Chief Fire Officer.'

The man's introduction surprised Darryl. He was tall, but of slight build. His firefighter's uniform hung off him as though it was two sizes too big. Not the regular physique you would expect of a firefighter. He had tucked his helmet under one arm, and a hand that seemed too big for the rest of his body held his gloves.

'The fire is out now,' the man continued, 'but I'm afraid the water damage will be just as significant. It's mainly localised to the hall and could have been a lot worse. Can you fill me in on what happened?'

While he was speaking, Eleanor had appeared at Darryl's side and took hold of his arm. Her pale face mirrored his own. Darryl explained how he had woken first, now grateful for the uncomfortable sofa that had kept him from falling into a deep sleep. He explained how he had woken Eleanor first and discovered that the fire was at the front door.

'That makes sense from what we can see at the moment,' said the fire officer. 'We'll know more after a full investigation.'

'But there was something there,' Darryl suddenly remembered. He tried to bring back the vision in his head of when he had first looked towards the front door and seen the fire. 'There was something on the doormat. I don't know what it was, there was no shape to it, just a mass. But it was a mass of something that wasn't there when we went to bed last night.' The realisation of what he was saying hit him. 'Was this deliberate?'

'I'm afraid it's too early to give any theories at this stage. We need to investigate before anything can be confirmed.'

~

Eleanor sat silently in the back of the police car. Dazed and unfocused. After everything that had happened, and now this. Darryl had gone back to studying the damage from the opposite side of the lane, as much as he could. Unable to rest.

A rustling sound brought Eleanor back to the moment. Amelia, who had been sitting by her side, fidgeted in her silver blanket.

'Would it be possible—' Amelia said. 'I know it's not a good time for you, but—'

Eleanor could see she didn't want to finish the question, and she didn't need to. To her, her sister's death was still the priority of her visit and the sun had now risen enough for them to see the garden.

'I don't think we can now,' she said sympathetically.

Amelia's eyes welled, though she tried to hide it. Eleanor understood her need for some kind of closure. She had come so far and was so close. Eleanor peered through the windows of the car. Even though she herself had no energy or inclination to move, she couldn't let Amelia come all this way for nothing. She hesitated, knowing this was the wrong thing to do, but with most of the activity at the front of the house, she might be able to give Amelia the closure she needed.

'Come on,' she said.

She forced herself out of the car. Their movement alerted the paramedic nearby and Eleanor announced their need for some fresh air and to stretch their legs. The paramedic returned to their paperwork with a friendly warning of staying near to the car so he could monitor them.

The two women, clinging on to their blankets, wandered nonchalantly around the driveway area. Eleanor cursed the gravel with every footstep. As they moved closer to the back of the house, making sure nobody was looking, they hurried together round the corner and out of the line of sight. They made their way round the back of the house and towards the area where the patio had been hiding the body of Jennifer Nightingale.

Police tape still cordoned off the area, but the tent that had covered the grave was now gone. Though they had come this far, Eleanor still didn't dare cross the police tape and enter the cordoned area, but the burial site was only ten metres away, close enough for Amelia to see.

'This is it?' Amelia asked with surprise as they approached.

'I'm afraid so. The tree was pushing up the patio slabs,' Eleanor explained, but Amelia interrupted before she could say anymore.

'A cherry tree. She loved cherry trees.' Amazement filled her voice. 'We had one in the garden when we were growing up. A huge one that we used to climb. We'd spend hours making up stories about fairy families that lived there. It's strange, but it somehow brings me comfort that she's been next to a cherry tree for all these years.'

'If it wasn't for that tree, she may never have been found,' Eleanor said.

They stood in quiet reflection together, watching the shadows of the branches move slowly across the broken earth as the sun rose. Small patches of sunlight danced in the breeze on the upturned soil.

Eleanor's gaze fell on the pile of patio slabs she had created.

She had planned to use the good ones to place a bench on. The tree roots had only broken a couple. The rest had been pushed and lifted until they jutted unevenly. They were nice slabs but there wasn't enough for a decent sized table and chairs. Maybe for a bench facing out over the farmer's fields and beyond. That had been the original idea, but now Eleanor wasn't so sure she wanted to keep them at all. There would always be the morbid association of a body being hidden underneath. Taking another look at them now, though, they seemed familiar.

She left Amelia's side and moved closer to the pile of slabs, examining them carefully, trying to remember where she had seen them before. The smooth stone, the warm honey colour and sleek surface. Thoughts churning through her mind. Was it before or after she'd found Jenny? Maybe it was simply a subconscious memory from seeing them in the garden before. She turned back to Amelia with a sigh of frustration. Tears were rolling down Amelia's face. Eleanor pushed her thoughts aside and took Amelia's hand, squeezing it comfortingly.

Amelia wiped her eyes with her other hand and gave a gentle smile. Her search was at an end.

～

'Hi, Dad. Mum said you were trying to get hold of us.'

The sound of his daughter's voice on the other end of the phone brought great relief to Darryl. He had only just hung up from calling the pub for rooms when his phone rang. A call from Kathy was a welcome distraction.

'I'm guessing it's actually Alex you want, though,' Kathy continued.

'Don't be like that. You know I love to hear from both of you.'

'Yeah, but it's not me that's dropping out of Uni, is it?'

Her tone was serious. Darryl guessed she wasn't too keen on

the idea either. 'I guess you do have a point there,' he conceded. 'Do you know why she's dropping out, or even where she is?'

'You know I'm not going to tell you that, don't you?'

Her loyalty to her sister was as strong as Darryl knew it would be, and no amount of persuasion would sway her.

'Yeah, I know, but I need to tell your mother something.' His voice automatically returned to the familiar disdain when referring to Rachel.

'Dad,' Kathy implored.

'Sorry, love. At least tell me she's alright. We just want to help.'

'She just needs a bit of time to sort things out.'

'What things?' Darryl asked, scenarios playing in his head. Wedding plans? An abortion?

'Don't worry about it, Dad.'

'I do worry. It's my job to worry.'

'Well, don't,' Kathy snapped. There was a moment's silence before she continued. 'I'm sorry, Dad. I...' Her voice drifted off.

'Come on, you know I'd do anything for you.' A warning had flared. It would take a lot for Kathy to snap like that.

Alex had always been the one that craved attention. And, because of it, Kathy was often overlooked. She could even have seen it as being ignored. Too busy dealing with Alex's tantrums, Alex's mishaps, Alex's mischievousness to worry themselves over their other daughter. Kathy was always the one that sat quietly watching, never causing any trouble. Darryl loved both his girls and sometimes he was concerned Kathy didn't believe that.

'I will try and get Alex to call you, but it's not down to me to deal with her issues.'

'You're right, I know. And it's not fair that you're stuck in the middle.'

'Yeah—'

She sounded like she was about to say more, but Darryl had to cut her off. DCI Carl Hanson had pulled up outside the front of the house. Blocked from going any further by the fire engine in the road and the driveway already full of vehicles.

'Look, love, it's difficult to talk now. I'll call you later. Our house has just been burnt down,' he added with a satirical laugh.

'What? What happened? Are you and Eleanor OK?'

Darryl smiled at the reference to Eleanor. They hadn't yet met, but Kathy had accepted her from the start. 'We're both fine, but the house isn't looking too good. I'll call you again soon, OK?'

'Sure, bye, Dad.'

'Love you,' he said and hung up, immediately regretting it. He hadn't spoken to Kathy for weeks, and now he was hanging up on her when it was clear something was troubling her. He consoled himself with the thought that at least he had a good reason for it, and he made a silent promise that he would call her back as soon as he could. Pushing his guilt aside, he greeted the DCI as he climbed out of his car.

∼

'Excuse me, ladies, you shouldn't be here.'

Eleanor jumped at the thin, reedy voice behind her. The chief fire officer who had introduced himself as Richard Atkins on his arrival had exited the house through the back door.

'I'm sorry it was my fault,' Amelia said quickly. 'I made her show me where my sister...' Amelia's voice broke off into sobs.

'I'm afraid we still can't allow you to be here. Please,' the fire officer extended an arm and ushered them back towards the driveway.

Eleanor, her arm comfortingly around Amelia's shoulders,

guided her gently as they inched their way along the grassy path.

They were nearing the corner of the house when Eleanor heard Darryl's voice.

'Come on, you know I'd do anything for you.' His tone was soft and loving.

Eleanor came to a sudden halt, though at their slow pace it would have been hardly noticeable. The woman from the cafe immediately came into mind and sickness rose in Eleanor's throat.

'You're right, I know. And it's not fair that you're stuck in the middle. Look, love, it's difficult to talk now. I'll call you later...' His voice drifted away with the crunch of slow footsteps on the gravel.

They turned the corner in time for Eleanor to see Darryl hanging up from his phone call and walking towards Carl Hanson, who was climbing out of his car.

Flustered, she tried to act as if nothing was wrong. Nothing other than finding their home on fire in the middle of the night.

'Mrs Garrett, if you wouldn't mind, I'd like to speak with both you and Mr Westwood,' the fire officer said as they approached the two men. 'It's not good news, I'm afraid, but I'd be surprised if you hadn't guessed that.' He turned his attention mainly to Eleanor. Perhaps experience had taught him bad news should be told directly to the woman of the household. 'You won't be able to move back into the house until we have completed a full investigation, and a structural survey will need to be done. You will need to find other arrangements.'

'Can we go in and collect a few things?' Eleanor asked.

'I'm afraid not. For one thing, I wouldn't like to trust the safety of your stairs.'

'Our bedroom is downstairs,' she added quickly. She had

already lost her house, she didn't want to be left with absolutely nothing.

The fire officer hesitated, as though thinking about whether it was worth the risk.

'The roof is leaking and we're having to use the dining room as our bedroom at the moment. It's even at the back of the house too, so we won't to go anywhere near the front—'

'OK, OK,' Richard conceded. 'I'll come in with you now to grab a few bits, as long as we can steer clear of the main damaged areas. But, you must understand, if at any point I think it's unsafe, we turn round and come right back out again.'

Amelia only had a few possessions with her that Eleanor offered to collect. And so, she returned to the shelter of the paramedic's car, while Darryl and Eleanor went back into the house via the back door.

In a line, the three of them entered the house. The chief fire officer leading the way, Darryl second and Eleanor behind.

'Who were you on the phone to?' Eleanor asked as they entered through the back door. The kitchen showed evidence of smoke and water covered the floor. But the door between the kitchen and the hallway had kept out the worst.

'The pub in the village. I could tell we wouldn't be able to stay here, so I rang them on the off-chance to see if they had any rooms, and we're in luck.'

That didn't sound like the conversation she had heard, but all thoughts of Darryl's call disappeared from Eleanor's mind once she entered the hallway. Every surface from floor to ceiling was black. The fire left only remnants of the boxes that had remained in the hallway, still waiting to be unpacked. Darryl faltered at the sight of the front door. A damp, black, charred mass. He had always had a strong emotional attachment to that door. He had spent hours examining the carvings, the wood grain, the incidental marks that meant nothing to anyone other than an archaeologist. But even Eleanor could tell they couldn't save it. She placed her hand on his arm in sympathy.

'I'm sorry about the door,' she whispered.

'I had already accepted that it was past repair from what I could see outside. We're OK though,' he continued, putting his arm around her and pulling her close. 'That's what we need to focus on right now,' he said, a gentle smile on his lips. 'This could have been so much worse.'

She nodded silently before he pulled away, and they followed the fire officer into their make-shift bedroom.

They grabbed a couple of suitcases, threw in some clothes and toiletries, and left the room together. They stopped at the end of the hallway and looked around at the devastation. Piles of ash lay sodden from the water hoses where the boxes used to be. Wet filth smothered the flagstone floor. Evidence of smoke damage extended along the hall walls and up the stairs.

'I think Amelia's right,' Darryl said. 'It wasn't some mysterious boyfriend that killed Jenny and then disappeared from the village. Someone local killed her and that someone doesn't like us asking questions.'

12

It was still early when Eleanor, Darryl, and Amelia arrived at the Cat and Kitten pub, carrying only the minimal amount of items they could survive with. As they hadn't been able to go upstairs, that was mainly clothes. Darryl ducked under a couple of low beams as they dragged their suitcases through to the stairs. On their way through, Eleanor overheard a quiet conversation between Carl and the landlord, asking for him to keep an eye open for anything suspicious for the duration of their stay. The DCI had briefly explained before entering that the landlord had recently retired from being a police detective himself and understood the situation only too well.

'You'll need to come into the station to give formal statements,' Carl said to the three of them. 'But get some sleep now. It can wait till later. I'll leave a message with Tom,' he indicated the landlord, 'as to when I need you in.'

The landlord showed Amelia a room she could rest and clean up in, and, after being shown to their room, Eleanor and Darryl unpacked slowly and silently. It was a long, listless morning. Exhausted from the night's events, they both fell asleep until a soft knocking on their door a few hours later. It was already past lunchtime, and the kitchen was about to close.

The dining area had been quiet when they arrived. The remnants of family lunch covered most of the tables. Dirty plates and half-eaten children's meals, much of it on the floor. Gravy drips and a mixture of custard and ice-cream drops across the tables. Two teenage waitresses busied themselves after a regular Saturday lunchtime rush.

The three were now slumped at a table tucked in a corner. Their food in front of them. The sedentary group sat silently while their meals turned cold, forks held loosely in their hands as they picked aimlessly. The dark beams and faded wallpaper that surrounded them kept the sunlight at bay, and their little corner of the pub felt as gloomy as their spirits.

'So, what now?' Eleanor asked. Tom had passed on the message from DCI Hanson, and they still had several hours until they needed to be at the station to give their statements.

The smell of disinfectant and the efficient swish of cleaning cloths, as the waitresses wiped down the tables surrounding them, replaced the clatter of dirty crockery being cleared.

'I need to go home this evening,' said Amelia. 'I have work tomorrow.'

'What do you do?' Darryl's voice was flat and uninterested.

'Nothing really, I'm just a faceless member of staff in a large department store.'

'Don't say that,' Eleanor implored, almost grateful to have her thoughts shifted and focused on something other than the house. 'Don't even think it.'

'I'd never thought about it before, but it's true and it suited me.' There was no pity in her voice, only a sense of resignation. 'Jenny was my life. I only worked to fund my search for her. I don't have a partner or hobbies. What am I going to do now?'

Eleanor laid down her fork and placed her hand on

Amelia's. The feeling of losing someone so close, the pain, the guilt, was all too well known.

'You're going to take some time to grieve for her, and then you're going to look around you and find that life is still moving on. You did everything you possibly could for her and now it's time for you.'

'I had always imagined a grand reunion between us when I would finally track her down and hold her in my arms,' Amelia said, with a strained voice. Her eyes, already bloodshot, couldn't hold back her tears any longer. She snatched up her room key from the table and disappeared back upstairs. Eleanor fought against the urge to chase after her, but there was only so much she could do. She picked up her fork and continued picking at her meal, more for something to do than because she was hungry.

The pub, now welcoming early afternoon customers, was filling again. After a few silent minutes Eleanor looked up and saw the postman, Shaun, leaning against the bar staring at her. No hint of reservation about him as he displayed himself on his bar stool.

'Maybe he did it,' Eleanor said quietly to Darryl.

Darryl looked up and followed Eleanor's eye line behind him. Shaun held up his pint glass in a cheers motion and Darryl gave a polite smile back, but quickly turned back to Eleanor.

'Maybe he tried it on with Jenny,' Eleanor continued, her mind imagining the scenario as if it was happening in front of her. 'She resisted, fought back, and things went a bit too far. Then he'd need to hide the evidence. Remember how he laughed when I pulled away? Women mean nothing to him.'

'What about his wife?' Darryl suggested. 'He makes no secret of his philandering. Maybe Jenny *didn't* resist, and Alison was jealous. But, then again, we don't know if they were married or even together back then. A lot happens in twenty years.'

'What if they weren't together but Alison wanted to be?' Eleanor suddenly felt hungry, and her knife and fork did what they were created for, instead of just playing with the food. 'If Jenny was in the way, Alison could have seen her as a threat.' She took a large mouthful of her lasagne. 'Though if Jenny was as afraid of men as Amelia says she was, that doesn't seem likely,' she continued thoughtfully.

'If we carry on like this,' Darryl said, 'we're going to find everybody in the village a suspect.'

'And so they are.'

'You're really getting into this now, aren't you?' Darryl sniggered.

'Amelia deserves to know what happened. It's like they buried her under that patio, along with Jenny. And one thing is for certain, we must be on the right track for someone to be going to such lengths to get rid of us.'

'On the right track.' Darryl repeated also tucking into his meal. 'We're not on any track.'

'Of course we are. It must be something to do with the school.'

'Or the postman... or his wife.' Darryl laughed. 'Maybe someone has just taken exception to us.'

Eleanor frowned.

'Let's face it, they're a bit late. We've already found the body,' he went on. 'Why would somebody be trying to scare us away now? Or kill us, for that matter? If we hadn't been sleeping in the lounge, we may not have woken in time.'

'No.' Eleanor shook her head frantically. 'It has to be connected. I think we're getting close to something. So, who else do we know was around at the time? Stella must have said something useful in all her babbling the other day. I must admit I sort of zoned out or tried to. Can you remember anything?' she asked.

'She said something about them being friends from school,' Darryl said thoughtfully.

'Who exactly?' Eleanor pushed her cleared plate aside and reached for a paper serviette off the table, and a pen from her bag.

Darryl pushed his empty plate next to Eleanor's and, with his elbows on the table, he put his head in his hands, thinking.

Eleanor wrote and underlined *list of suspects* at the top of the serviette.

'Do you have to give it a title? It's not as if we're going to forget what it is.'

'We'll start with Shaun.' Eleanor scrawled down the name, pointedly ignoring Darryl's remark, 'and Stuck-up Stella.'

A waitress arrived at their table while she was writing, and removed their empty plates. Eleanor quickly pulled the serviette out of sight and casually ordered two coffees.

'Stella,' Darryl said thoughtfully. 'She was talking about - Becky. It was Becky who she had been friends with at school. I had the feeling she included Alison in that, too.'

Eleanor added *Becky* and *Alison* to her list.

'Susan, the school Secretary,' Eleanor said as she wrote her name underneath. 'She was around then, too.'

Darryl was still focusing on trying to remember if there was anything relevant from Stella's deluge.

'She said she and DCI Hanson — Carl,' he corrected himself, 'had been married for an umpteen number of years, so I think we can safely assume he was around then, too.'

Eleanor wrote *DCI Carl Hanson*.

'Though he was with us when someone broke in upstairs,' Darryl continued.

'Which brings up the point that whoever broke in must have been fast to outrun him.' Eleanor chewed thoughtfully on the end of her pen. 'I remember,' she suddenly squealed.

Those in the bar turned to stare at her. She smiled apologetically back at them before they returned to their murmured conversations in the afternoon's peacefulness.

Eleanor screwed up the serviette and threw it at Darryl as he laughed at her embarrassment.

'Hey, we need that,' he said as he straightened out the napkin, unsuccessfully trying to hold back his laughter.

'When I took Amelia,' Eleanor continued, ignoring him, 'to the place where...'

'Yes,' Darryl finished, signifying he understood, and she didn't need to say the words while the waitress served their coffees.

'I recognised the patio slabs. I knew I had seen them before, but I couldn't remember where.'

'And now you remember,' he said.

'At the school,' Eleanor revealed excitedly.

Darryl let out a quick burst of laughter as she stared at him as though he should understand, but he was having a hard time seeing the relevance. 'So, you think there may be another body under their patio?'

'No, of course not. But it's another connection with the school. Maybe the people who laid that patio took some slabs and used them to cover...' Eleanor waved her hands in the air as though covering something in front of her. The scene became more farcical by the minute.

'It's a bit of a long shot. It may not have been laid around the same time to start with.'

'I think it was. Will said that they had laid it shortly before he got there and that's when Jenny went missing.' Eleanor's enthusiasm grew. 'I've got to ring Carl and tell him.' She grabbed her bag from the floor.

'Do you really think that's necessary?' Darryl asked.

'Definitely. It all centres round that school.' Eleanor rummaged in her bag for her phone and DCI Hanson's card.

'Eleanor, I think you're getting a bit over-excited.'

Eleanor turned and looked at him sternly. 'We have to do something.'

He said no more. Eleanor was determined. He relaxed back in his chair and watched as she entered the number on her phone.

'Hi, can I speak with DCI Hanson, please? Yes, it's Eleanor Garrett.'

Darryl and Eleanor sat in silence while they put her call through. Eleanor uncomfortably avoiding Darryl's eyes.

'Mrs Garrett,' Darryl heard clearly in the quiet of the pub. 'How can I help you?'

'I don't know if it's of any help to you, but I've just realised that the patio slabs that were used to cover Jenny's — I mean Miss Nightingale's, no, Miss Starling's body—'

'She's Miss Nightingale on the records, now.' Carl laughed at her confusion.

'Well, the patio slabs are also at the school.'

'I should imagine they're in a lot of places, Mrs Garrett. It's a popular style, but thank you for your observation.'

'Maybe so,' she continued, 'but it's where she worked, and I believe that they originally meant the patio area at the school to be bigger. Do you see the connection? It could have been that some of the slabs went missing specifically to hide Miss Nightingale.'

'What makes you think that, can I ask?'

Darryl flinched slightly at the DCI's tone. Her meddling didn't amuse him.

'It was something Will Cowley mentioned. He said it was a shame that the school had laid its patio without knowing how big it was going to become. That he would have laid a bigger patio right from the start.'

Darryl watched, quietly amused, as her face dropped with the realisation of how feeble the idea was.

'Maybe they were going to make it bigger,' she went on. 'it's just that someone ran off with a pile of their slabs.'

A brief silence followed Eleanor's theory before DCI Hanson spoke.

'Will Cowley always has much bigger ideas than are strictly necessary for such a small school.' His tone had changed to one of sympathy. He was humouring her. 'Those slabs are everywhere, so I really don't hold out much hope, but I'll look into it.'

'Thank you,' she said subdued, and she hung up. 'Go on, tell me what an idiot I am. Why didn't you stop me?'

'And ruin my fun.' Darryl grinned behind his coffee cup.

Eleanor picked up her pen and snatched at the crumpled serviette, returning to the list of names. 'Anyone else you can remember?' she snapped at Darryl.

'Well, of course, there's Mr wandering eyes over there,' said Darryl, reining in his laughter.

'He's at the top of the list.' Eleanor glanced over at him, still at the bar, but he was now, thankfully, looking the other way.

To Darryl's surprise, Eleanor suddenly screwed the serviette in her hand.

'Don't let Amelia know what we're doing,' she whispered. 'She needs to think it's over. She needs to move on.'

He looked curiously at Eleanor for a moment until Amelia appeared from behind him and returned to her seat.

'I have an idea,' Eleanor suddenly exclaimed. 'Would you like to see her?' she asked Amelia.

Amelia shook her head, bewildered. 'I don't understand.'

'Jenny, would you like to see Jenny? There is a tea-room in

Northwood Gate that has lots of photographs from years ago. There are pictures of Jenny there,' Eleanor explained.

'Of Jenny?' Amelia whispered. 'From when she lived here?'

'It may help you move on with your own life if you can see how happy she was while she was here. I don't know why I didn't think of it before.'

'Yes, yes, I would love to see her.' Though her smile was broad, her eyes were, again, full of tears.

13

The journey to Northwood Gate was silent. Nervous anticipation filled the car. Darryl remembered the photographs round the tea-room where he had sat with Rachel and wondered if that was where they were heading now. As if his conversation with Rachel didn't weigh heavily enough on his conscience. Soon. He'd be able to tell Eleanor soon. He put her sudden willingness to investigate down to being a useful distraction. With so much happening outside of her control, there was a need to focus on something she felt she could do.

As they walked along the street, getting closer to the tea-room, Darryl's nerves twitched. He had been right. It was the same one, and he hung back, hesitantly. It was almost empty as they entered and the woman who had served him yesterday, dressed in an old-fashioned black and white waitress uniform, appeared from the kitchen to greet them.

'Hello again,' she said to Eleanor with a nervous laugh.

Darryl and Eleanor had been to Northwood Gate town a few times over the last few weeks, but he was certain he hadn't been to this tea-room before, not before Rachel. How did this woman know Eleanor? But, too concerned with being recognised himself, he turned his face away and occupied himself with the photographs around the walls while Eleanor ordered the drinks.

'I hope you don't mind, but this lady,' Eleanor indicated Amelia, 'is Miss Starling's sister.'

The woman stared at Amelia; the blood drained from her face as though she was looking at a ghost.

'I know you have some photographs of Miss Starling and we just wanted to have a look, if we may,' Eleanor continued.

'Of course,' the woman whispered. 'Please, help yourself.' She rushed off to the kitchen, mumbling something about getting their drinks.

Amelia had already seen a photograph of Jenny during the conversation. Her face towards the sun; her eyes closed in the warmth. It drew Amelia forwards through a daze, and Eleanor followed. Darryl too, nervous about seeing the real Jennifer Nightingale, but his curiosity was stronger. Maybe it would help remove the vision of his first encounter with her, or what was left of her. In the photograph, he saw a woman in her mid to late twenties. Her profile stressed the similarity between the two sisters. The small, rounded nose and slightly pointed chin. An attractive woman with a long slender neck.

'This scar,' Amelia showed a mark behind Jenny's ear. 'This was her husband. He was threatening to slit her throat with a broken glass during one of his drunken outbursts.'

'There's no denying that this is Jenny, then,' Eleanor said.

'No, this is my Jenny. And she's happy.' Tears welled again.

Eleanor put her arm around Amelia's shoulders, while Darryl, slightly uncomfortable, looked around at the other photographs. After his initial annoyance of the distraction away from the architectural features of the building the last time he was here, he had become intrigued by them. Old photographs that may lead to some clue as to who was living here twenty years ago. Though this wasn't the time to ask those questions,

Eleanor was right. Amelia needed to move on and if she knew they were investigating, it wouldn't help. So, instead, he searched several local pictures, particularly those of Bramblemere. He came across a photograph of a woman that looked like Jenny with a small child. The woman crouched, so they were face to face, and laughing together.

'Is this her, too?' he asked. Amelia needed a distraction. Some help to remember the good times. 'She looks like she had a way with kids.'

Amelia tore her eyes away from the previous photograph and smiled through her tears. 'Yes, that's her. It doesn't surprise me at all that she became a teacher. She always loved kids.'

The waitress brought their drinks to their table, but Amelia kept searching, drink in hand. Darryl had waited for the waitress to return to the kitchen before he moved to sit at the table with his coffee. But then the waitress arrived with a small bowl of sugar. She smiled politely at Darryl, faltering as she placed the pot on the table as recognition scanned across her face.

'I- I've brought some sugar.' She turned quickly and returned to the kitchen, glancing at Eleanor on the way.

She remembers me, he thought. *Oh great.* This was not how he wanted Eleanor to find out. He thought about how he could approach the subject of Rachel and Alex. Subconsciously, he reached for the jewellery box in his jacket pocket. *Oh yeah, and that.*

After a couple of minutes, Eleanor came to join him.

'I'm glad I remembered this place,' she said quietly and sipped at her coffee. 'I think she's going to be alright.'

He watched Eleanor as her eyes followed Amelia round the room. The waitress hesitantly joined Amelia and pointed out the relevant photographs, chatting quietly together. The pity in Eleanor's eyes overflowed. She knew the reality of losing someone you love so much. Not just the death, but the subsequent pain that followed. How quick you are to blame yourself for their death; how loss is a physical pain, not just an emotional one. Darryl remembered clearly how, when they first met, she was struggling just with living day to day, and how her guilt was crippling her. A preposterous and senseless guilt, but logical to her.

'Eleanor, I wanted to—'

'Have you seen the photograph of our house?' she interrupted. She got up from the table and rushed closer to a photograph at the back of the tea-room.

She's going to have to sit still at some point, Darryl thought, and he got up and followed her to the picture, expecting a tiny image of the house in amongst a great landscape of rolling hills. Instead, he was drawn in to an image of a large, beautiful house. The central character of the scene. Their home. Wanting to touch the image as though it was the actual object, he could barely breathe at its splendour. There was no rot around the windows, no overgrown brambles. It was just as beautiful as he had always known it would be. Whether it would ever be that way again seemed highly unlikely now.

'It's time for me to get to the police station now,' Amelia said from behind them. 'Thank you so much for bringing me here. I can't tell you what a comfort it's been to see that at least the last few years of her life were happy ones.'

'We'll take you round there,' Eleanor offered.

'Honestly, there's no need. The walk will do me good. The owner has just given me directions, and it's only a five-minute walk through a short-cut. She's also given me this picture of Jenny.'

Amelia was clutching the photograph of Jenny, warming her face in the sun.

'Apparently, it went missing a few years ago, and they had to replace it. I think Connor may have taken it.'

'Connor? That was the private investigator?' Darryl clarified.

'Yes. Maybe it was this picture that brought him to this part of the country. He would easily have recognised her from this.' She paused while taking another look at her long-lost sister. 'Well, I've taken enough of your time already. Thank you again, and I hope we meet under better circumstances one day. You've been very generous to me and you don't deserve what's happened. I hope you find out what started—'

Eleanor stood, interrupting Amelia, cutting off any discussion about the house.

'You just get home and start a new life for yourself,' she said, giving Amelia a hug.

They said their goodbyes and watched Amelia leave the tea-room, her rucksack on her back. Darryl, glad that they were now alone, sat back at the table expecting Eleanor to sit with him, but she continued looking at the photographs.

'Eleanor, your coffee's getting cold,' he said.

But instead of joining him, she took her coffee with her.

The tea-room was now empty other than the owner, adding the final touches to the cleared tables. Darryl's voice rose with frustration.

'Eleanor—'

'This is you, isn't it?' Eleanor said to the tea-room owner, pointing to a photograph of a group of school children. Not standing smartly as they would normally be for a school photo, but relaxed, ready to run off and cause mischief. 'You're unmistakable with that long hair. Who are the others?' she asked with a sideways glance towards Darryl. 'People often don't leave small villages. Are they still local?'

The waitress walked over to Eleanor, her shoulders dropping with an enormous sigh as she looked at the picture. 'I have to admit, this is one of my favourites. I know it's pure indulgence on my part, but these were the good old days when we had no worries. Yes, you're right, that's me. This was taken on our last day at that school. It's a primary school, so we were only eleven. This is Alison,' she pointed to the first girl in the row. 'She now has the village shop in Bramblemere, and this,' she continued along the row of children, 'is Shaun, her now husband. He's the postman. You've probably seen him around the village.'

'Yes, we've met them,' Darryl said, joining them and also examining the photograph. 'Is this one Stella?'

'Yes, you've met her too, then.'

Her curly blonde hair was unmistakable, and even back then, she was much shorter than all the others.

'This is Carl. You wouldn't believe it from this photo, but he's a detective chief inspector now.' The boy she was pointing at was scruffier than the rest of the children, with long, straggly hair. His school shirt hanging out of his trousers and covered in mud patches. He stood holding hands with his neighbour.

'And the girl next to him?' Eleanor asked.

'Becky, she now teaches at that school in Bramblemere where the photo was taken. And then there's me on the end. I'm Jo, by the way.'

Darryl and Eleanor introduced themselves.

The photograph directly underneath was the one Darryl had seen on his previous visit. A group of six, outside the same school, and lined up as before, dated twenty years ago.

'Is this the same group?' Darryl asked.

'Yes, taken a few years later. We stuck together for the next few years, right through secondary school. '

The group stood in the same places as they were in the first photograph. Alison and Shaun were the first two on the left, but now holding hands. Stella was almost lost in the middle. Carl and Becky stood together, his arm around her waist and her head resting on his shoulder. Then came Jo on the far end. Her hair was no longer waist length, but just below the shoulders.

'Twenty years ago,' Darryl said, pointedly reading the date.

'Yes, yes, it was. I had my nineteenth birthday just a few days earlier.'

'Around the time Miss Starling went missing?' Eleanor asked.

'Yes, that's right. I was working at the school with Becky at the time. Poor Becky, she was having an awful time. She was suddenly left with the class on her own until they could get someone else in. Her mother had multiple sclerosis and had recently had a nasty fall, and then she had her heart broken when her boyfriend ran off on her.'

'Carl?' Eleanor asked. 'They look very happy together here.'

'No, not Carl. She broke up with Carl very soon after this was taken. Some new chap had come and swept her off her feet. It was a real whirlwind affair, as they say, but it only lasted a couple of weeks, if that. I was probably the closest one to her at the time, working at the school too, and even I never got to meet him. I guess it was a pretty bad time for all of us. My dad walked out; I don't think Carl ever got over Becky leaving him; though Stella did pretty well. She'd had a crush on Carl ever since time began. Never imagined they'd ever get together, though, let alone marry.'

'What about Alison and Shaun?' Eleanor asked.

She gave a burst of laughter. 'Shaun was quite shaken up by it, too. It devastated him that Miss Starling had left the village without him. He had a bit of a thing for her. One of those older women out of reach things, if you know what I mean, even though he was with Alison at the time. But then again, Shaun tends to have a thing for most women. I'm sorry, I shouldn't say things like that.'

'Don't worry, we've met him. We know exactly what you mean.' Eleanor pulled a face.

'Don't take it personally. It's just a silly game they play.

Anyway, we had all started to go our separate ways with work and such likes and we didn't see each other often. It was only because my mother insisted on this photograph to match the other one that it happened at all. She could be very persuasive when she wanted to be.'

'You worked at the school?' Darryl said, picking up on another, though admittedly tenuous, connection with the school.

'Yes, I was a teaching assistant, like Becky, but we worked in different classrooms.'

'We were told everyone from the school had left the area since that time.' Darryl's interest stirred.

'That doesn't surprise me. I was only there six months. My time there has long been forgotten. I needed to come and help Mum here in the tea-room. Dad had walked out and left her, so...'

'Your daughter said, when I was in before, that your father was in charge of the investigation into Miss Starling's disappearance,' Eleanor said.

'Yes, that's right.' She seemed startled, but continued. 'A stressful job, as you can imagine. Then one day he just up and left. To be honest, the marriage wasn't too great to start with. Constant arguments. Dad spent less and less time at home. They tried to hide it from me but, well, kids aren't stupid. Anyway, after he left, Mum needed help, so I left the school and came to work here. Two years later, she died. She never really recovered, and here I've been ever since.' Her voice had become sullen with her story.

'I'm sorry to hear that,' Eleanor said.

'I only hope he found the peace he was looking for, but I'll never forgive him.' She smiled politely and left for the kitchen.

'We've brought back all those memories,' Eleanor said sadly.

'She's surrounded by those memories.' Darryl returned to their table.

A thought had struck him, and he couldn't help but see a comparison between Jo's story and Alex's situation. Jo had left work at the school as a result of her parents separating. Surely Alex's reason for dropping out of Uni couldn't have anything to do with the divorce, could it?

'I'm just going to pop to the ladies,' Eleanor said, and she headed for the corridor that led to the toilets and an outside area.

Darryl mulled over the implications of the divorce for Alex and Kathy. Or maybe not the divorce so much, but the years of arguing before it. Alex had always been confident in herself. Nothing seemed to phase her. Or maybe she was just good at hiding it. As Jo had said, kids aren't stupid. They would have known what was going on.

'Darryl, Darryl!'

A loud whisper jolted Darryl from his thoughts. Eleanor was pointing through a high window that ran down the side of the corridor. She mouthed something, but what was anyone's guess. She then continued along the corridor towards the ladies' room.

Intrigued, and with no one else around, Darryl went to look out the window. Something had caught Eleanor's attention out there. Outside was a small courtyard area, just enough room for three groups of table and chairs, and a few scattered empty plant pots. He couldn't be certain, but the patio looked like it was made from the same slabs.

'I'm afraid outside isn't available at the moment.'

Darryl jumped at Jo's arrival, carrying a tray full of small, white ceramic salt and pepper pots.

'We've only just had the patio laid and we're still finishing off out there,' she continued, placing her tray on one of the tables.

She took one of each of the pots and placed them in the centre of the table and moved on to the next.

Darryl's broad grin spread across his face.

'That's fine,' he said. 'I'm just being nosey.' He returned to his table, laughing at the idea of Eleanor's response.

'I'm sorry, but...' The waitress had turned back to Darryl. 'Were you in here yesterday? I'm usually very good with faces, but I don't remember you from when Eleanor was here before, and yet I'm sure I've seen you—'

'I was here, yes... with another woman. My ex-wife,' Darryl added quickly with a nervous laugh. He glanced towards the toilet door, not wanting Eleanor to hear of it like this.

'Forgive me, I didn't mean to pry. I thought I was going crazy. I was certain I had seen you before. I just couldn't place you.'

Darryl struggled with the urge to ask when Eleanor had been in before, but thought it better to let Jo continue working before Eleanor emerged. Within seconds, Eleanor hurried back to her seat.

She leaned across the table and whispered, 'It's the same slabs. Surely that can't be a coincidence.'

'Why not?' Darryl asked. 'A lot of people have patios and those are nice slabs.' Darryl, his heart racing from his previous conversation with Jo, brought himself round to focus back on Eleanor and their investigation.

'Or Jo could have used some of their slabs to cover Jenny. She could even have stolen their slabs from the school.'

The clatter of the ceramic salt and pepper pots being placed on the wooden tables covered Eleanor's whispers before Jo returned to the kitchen.

'How big was this school patio going to be to have provided enough slabs for both here, our place and still have some left at the school?' he said sarcastically.

'But she worked there at the time. She could have been

stealing them and got caught. Maybe that's the real reason she left after six months.'

'Your imagination really does run wild, doesn't it? The same could be said for your teacher friend then, too. Maybe you'd better find out where Becky was living at the time. She could have the best patio yet,' he said, enjoying his secret.

'And,' Eleanor was clearly undeterred, 'that's why Jo's dad was so stressed. He knew his own daughter had done it. Instead of turning her in, he walked away. The lesser of two evils.'

'Do you really think she would kill for a few patio slabs?' Darryl asked.

Eleanor sat back, thinking. Looking round the room at all the photographs, she said, 'Her mum was a keen photographer. She took a lot of pictures of her. What if, when Jenny came along, her mum decided she wanted to photograph her instead of her own daughter?'

'Jealousy?' Darryl exclaimed. 'Over a few photographs?'

'She may have imagined a great modelling career until Miss Starling walked in and took over.'

'Why are you so fixated on the patio slabs, anyway?' Darryl asked. 'They could have nothing to do with it at all. They could be just a coincidence. Already in the garden and just in the right place at the right time.'

'Several reasons. The patio itself was in an odd position. Just stuck out on its own with the tree. It didn't look right. It also wasn't big enough to be of any use. Plus, also, it's the only clue we have. Why are you laughing at me?'

'There's only one problem.' Darryl couldn't hold back any longer.

'What?'

'These slabs are new. They have only just laid this patio.'

Eleanor opened her mouth to retaliate, but she had nothing

to come back with. She slumped back in her seat, crossing her arms in front of her. 'The theory is still sound,' she mumbled.

'The theory is questionable, and the evidence is non-existent.' They sat quietly for a moment, Darryl trying to hide his grin behind his coffee mug.

'What about the letters?' Eleanor asked.

Darryl looked at her quizzically.

'You were looking through Jenny's letters and postcards last night. Was there anything of interest in there? I was going to read through them today, but...' Eleanor's sentence trailed off. Her reason for not reading them was too obvious to mention.

'I didn't read much, but she wrote about finding her sanctuary and finally feeling safe. The people she worked with were kind, but she mentioned one person who she saw hanging around the house. He makes her nervous, but,' Darryl tried to recall the wording, 'but she knows he has a legitimate reason for being there and is gradually getting used to him. I think we can both guess who that means.'

'Shaun.' Eleanor gave a heavy sigh. 'The perks of being a postman.' She suddenly sat up with a strange, fixed smile. 'Don't look now but Stuck-up Stella and Carl are across the road. He must have finished Amelia's interview already.'

'Have they seen us?' asked Darryl.

'Sorry to say, but yes.' Eleanor gave a nod of recognition towards the window.

'Is she coming this way?' Darryl didn't dare turn to look.

'What do you think? Carl has gone off and left her to her own devices. Surely he should know better than to let her loose on the neighbourhood.'

'Let's go. We're all done here, aren't we?' Darryl stood. 'And it must be nearly time for our interviews. I'll go pay.' He turned and acknowledged Stella as though he hadn't known she was entering the tea-room. He then hurried to the back of the tea-room to pay before she had the chance to speak.

'I'm surprised to see you in here,' Stella said, approaching Eleanor, though continuing the sentence in a whisper and gesticulating towards Darryl, 'after the other day.'

Eleanor made a motion as if to say there was nothing to worry about. It was all a big misunderstanding.

'We were just leaving, I'm afraid.'

'To the police station?' Stella said. 'Carl told me what happened. How awful. You won't want to stay in our lovely little village at this rate.' She laughed with much more enthusiasm than was necessary or appropriate.

'It certainly seems like somebody doesn't want us here,' Eleanor said, more to herself than to Stella, which was just as well as Stella spoke over her with no inclination to want to hear what she may have to say.

'You're certainly keeping Carl busy. Running round night and day, I've never seen him so stressed.'

'I'm sorry we're making his life so difficult,' Darryl said with slight sarcasm as he returned from paying.

Jo had followed behind with a tray and began clearing their table.

'Thank you,' Eleanor said to her, 'for everything.'

'You're welcome,' Jo said. 'Sometimes it's nice to look again at some of these photographs. They tend to just blend into the background nowadays.'

'My usual cappuccino please, Jo,' Stella interrupted.

Her harshness surprised Eleanor. Even though Jo was a waitress, she was still her friend and didn't deserve to be ordered about like that.

'Anyway—' Stella started in a more gentle tone towards Eleanor, but Darryl interrupted loudly.

'Anyway, sorry to run off like this. Lovely to see you again,'

His voice loud and firm. Stella had no choice but to stop and listen. He hustled Eleanor out the door.

'Maybe we should actually talk to her,' Eleanor said once outside in the street. 'She knows more than anyone what's going on around here.'

'Do you really want to put yourself through that?' Darryl asked.

Eleanor didn't need to reply.

14

Darryl woke early Sunday morning. He tried to get back to sleep, but it was useless with so much running round his head. He thought about waking Eleanor, using the time to explain the situation about Rachel and Alex. But, watching her sleeping peacefully, he thought better of it. He had woken in the night and found her crying silently. It had only been just over a year since she had lost her husband and son, and she still cried for them from time to time. The night-time was always the worst. He had learnt that there was nothing he could do but hold her and hope that her nightmares would soon end. No words would soothe her, nothing but time could help her.

He crept out of bed and held his breath till he made it to the bathroom. He showered, dressed and, on returning to their one room, felt cramped and he longed to get out into the fresh air. The early sun glowed through the curtains. Their window, looking out over the green, was east facing and caught the full morning sun as it rose over the rooftops of the terraced cottages on the opposite side. Leaving for a walk, he crept out the door, praying the creaking of the over-sized iron hinges on the ancient oak door didn't wake Eleanor after all his efforts to be quiet. His last vision of her, as he pulled the door closed behind him, was one of peacefulness.

There was nearly an hour to go before he needed to leave for work, even though it was a Sunday. Working irregular days often had its advantages, but it also had its downsides. Weekends and school holidays are the busiest times for tourist dependant businesses. As a charitable trust, the Minstrel-Wood site was definitely classed as one of those, and so employees had to adapt. His heart sank at the thought of leaving Eleanor on her own in the pub all day, but he also guiltily looked forward to having something else to focus on. They had discussed it last night and Darryl had been on the verge of calling to let them know he wouldn't be in when Eleanor had talked him out of it. He was certain they wouldn't expect him to go in after what had happened. Despite that, a semblance of normality would do him good.

Outside, the morning was fresh with a slight mist hanging over the village pond. As he strolled across the green, the dew soaking through his trainers, he saw the bakery van pull up outside the village shop. His stomach rumbled at the thought of warm, fresh bread, and his footsteps quickened.

'Morning, Alison,' he said as he approached the counter, giving a good morning nod to the bakery van driver as he passed on his way out. The smell of the bread warmed Darryl's soul as soon as he had entered the shop.

'Good morning. What can I get for you?' Alison said, arranging the newly arrived selection.

'I saw the bakery van and couldn't resist.'

'Nothing like freshly baked bread to start the day.' Alison made a quick glance towards the door that led through to the living quarters before continuing in more hushed tones. 'Do you know what happened the other night?'

Darryl looked at her curiously. 'Our house burnt down,' he said bluntly.

Alison gave a slight, embarrassed laugh and another quick glance towards the doorway. 'Of course, I'm so sorry to hear what happened. But, I was wondering if you know why? Was it faulty electrics? Let's face it, the electrics are probably so old by now, they could have short-circuited or something. A terrible thing to happen.'

'No, I'm afraid that's not what happened. We made sure we rewired the entire house when we first moved in.' It was ironic that Darryl had made the conscious decision that the electrics were one of the first things to be done. The last thing he wanted was for something to happen because of his own negligence. 'To be honest, I believe it was deliberate.'

Alison let out a squeak in shock.

'I saw something,' Darryl went on, 'it all happened so quick, but I saw something at the foot of the front door where the fire started, before it went up in flames.'

Alison's voice lowered, almost to a growl. 'It was in the middle of the night; you must have been tired. Could you have been mistaken?'

Darryl hardly heard the question through her defensive tone. 'No, I wasn't mistaken,' he said sternly. 'It was only for a second, but I'm certain there was something there.' Her demeanour made him wonder what she was insinuating. 'Why?'

She suddenly turned, gave a huge smile, and her attitude changed as quickly as the shake of her head. 'No reason, no reason. Just my insatiable curiosity.' She glanced again at the empty doorway in the awkward silence. 'I thought of joining the fire service once, you know,' she went on. An attempt to change the conversation's tone.

Darryl held back a laugh and raised his eyebrows with false interest. She didn't look like someone who could deal with the kind of things the fire service had to deal with, but then again, neither did Richard, and he was the chief. But she had sown a seed in his head and questions were bubbling.

'Only think about, or did you take it further?' he asked.

'I did quite a lot of the training and then got pregnant. The end of my career.'

'It didn't have to be,' Darryl said, trying to sound sympathetic as she had returned to her defensive tone. But on a more pragmatic side, thinking how she may not have joined the fire service but would still have enough training to be a pretty competent arsonist, and she certainly doesn't want anybody overhearing their conversation.

'I'm afraid it did. By the time the children had grown up and left home, I was in no fit state to be joining the fire service.'

She sounded bitter. How much of a temper did this woman hold? He said nothing other than his order for two plain croissants for Eleanor and a large almond croissant for himself.

His phone rang with the sound of a text while he paid. It was from Kathy.

Have spoken with Alex on your behalf and she wants to be left alone. Will contact you when she is ready xx

Darryl, grateful for the excuse to leave the shop, returned to the green to find a bench and enjoy his croissant. He struggled to get the conversation with Alison out of his head while he stared blankly at Kathy's text. Forcing himself, he made a mental note to tell Eleanor of Alison's suspicious behaviour, and pushed it out of his mind, turning his attention to a reply for Kathy. He bit into the warm, flaky croissant while gazing out over the village pond, thinking. He didn't want to drag Kathy into the middle of the whole sorry situation, and yet Kathy was probably the only person Alex would talk to.

> **Thanks but it's not fair for her to put you in the middle. Tell her to stop being a coward and call me. Would tell her myself but... xx**

He sat watching the morning mist melt away in the sun's warmth as it rose higher. His shoulders relaxed as it warmed his back. Slowly, the reflection of the blue sky revealed itself as the mist disappeared from the pond. Two sparrows took it in turn to perch on the end of the bench, waiting for croissant flakes to drop to the ground.

His phone didn't sound again until he was almost back at the pub.

> **She says she doesn't want a lecture. She'll ring you when she's ready. Now done my part, I'm finished xx**

Darryl's frustration with Alex grew, but he couldn't ask more of Kathy. He simply replied with,

> **You're the best. Love you xx**

Eleanor woke later than she would normally. Exhausted by the events of the last few days and a broken night's sleep. In the night's silence, her mind refused to settle and thoughts of Nick and Chris had seeped in. With no distractions to occupy her mind, it didn't take long for the tears to start. Vulnerable in the stillness of the dark. Creeping out of their bedroom had become a frequent event, and Darryl was none the wiser. But sometimes, like last night, there was nowhere to hide. At the beginning of their relationship, there were endless questions. He desperately wanted to help, but there was nothing he could do. Nothing that would make either of them feel any better. Now, several months later, it had become a familiar occurrence. There were no more questions and instead he would simply hold her till the tears stopped. During the day, they avoided the subject.

The light of the morning pushed those thoughts back into the recesses of her memory and she woke slowly, relishing her comfortable bed with clean sheets. She took in a long, slow, deep breath. Even the air she breathed was different somehow.

She pushed back the white sheets and put her feet on the floor. Bare feet on a thick, woolly rug. She wriggled her toes. The rug wasn't anything extravagant, but to her it was indulgence itself. She strolled over to the window and pushed back the curtains, letting the sun stream in and warm her face. The small individual squares of glass, fixed with a crosshatch of lead, were mostly ancient and thick, distorting the view of the village green outside. *I could get used to this,* she thought. Gazing at the distorted shapes of the trees opposite the pub, movement pulled her focus, and she saw Darryl crossing the lane towards the pub. In one hand, he held a small but bulky white paper bag. In his other hand was his phone. The distorted image was clear enough for Eleanor to see he was texting. He returned the phone to his pocket and disappeared from view as he neared the pub entrance below her. Eleanor didn't want to believe there was another woman, but there was no mistaking what she had seen. And the mysterious trip to the jewellers? Whatever he had bought, he hadn't given it to the woman in the tea-room. She had seen him feel his jacket where his inside pocket held something rectangular and hard. Maybe he was waiting for a particular occasion to give it to her. Or, could it be that the item wasn't for the other woman, but was, as Eleanor originally had thought, a ring for her? A ring to replace the one given to her by Nick? But that thought also brought a lump to her throat. Was the idea of marrying another man any better than that man having an affair? Remnants of guilt still hung heavily over her from moving on from Nick. Subconsciously, she twisted her wedding ring round and round her finger. The smoothness of the gold sliding between her thumb and forefinger. She caught herself and spun from the window, clenching her fists.

The door opened quietly, and Darryl's face drifted silently into view.

'You're awake,' he said and quickened his movements, charging into the room. 'I was up early. Didn't want to wake you so I went out for a walk.' He set the miniature kettle going and put coffee in a mug.

Eleanor let him ramble, quietly seething, wondering if he would mention the text.

'While I was out the bakery van pulled up at the shop and I thought you might like breakfast in bed with freshly baked,' he paused and felt the outside of the white paper bag before continuing, 'slightly warm croissants.'

Eleanor sat back on the bed and quietly watched him flit about.

'There's no plate,' he mumbled, scanning the room.

'That's fine. I'll eat them out of the bag. Are you joining me?'

'In a hurry, I'm afraid.' He gave Eleanor the bag of croissants and placed the coffee on the bedside table. 'I was out longer than intended and now I've got to rush to get to work.' He gave her a peck on the forehead and looked down at her. 'Are you sure you don't mind me going in? I'm sure they'll let me take a few days off.'

'There's no need,' Eleanor said, peering into the bag of croissants. The warm scent filled her nostrils. 'There's nothing that can be done and I'm just going to soak in the bath for as long as possible. No jam?'

'Sorry, didn't think about jam.' Darryl slung his bag over his shoulder and looked around the room, searching. 'And a quick word of warning. I've just had an extraordinary conversation with Alison. Very shifty-looking if you ask me, and she was asking questions about the fire.' He felt his pockets and continued searching, lifting various items; his book on the bedside table, a pack of local interesting information provided with the room, sending the loose sheets across the floor. 'Also, she was training to be a firefighter before her kids came along, so she'd know all about arson and the best ways to go about it,' he continued as he picked up the papers and stuffed them back inside the card wallet. 'We may need a closer look at her for any motives.' He felt his pockets for a second time. 'Where are my keys?'

Eleanor pointed to them on his bedside table, behind the lamp. It always amazed her how even here, with not much space, he could still manage to lose his keys.

'Thanks. So, steering clear of the shop today would probably be a good idea. Got to run, bye.' Darryl grabbed his car keys and ran out the door.

He left Eleanor feeling like a quick, blustery storm had just swept its way through the room. A very obliging storm serving coffee and croissants, but a storm none the less.

'Steer clear of the shop? I don't think so.' She put her mind to thinking about how she could find out more about Alison. Darryl's text pushed to the back of her mind.

She ripped down the sides of the paper bag to create a plate that would at least catch the flakes of pastry that fell as she bit into them. *Alison. Could she have had a motive for killing Jenny Nightingale?*

Suddenly, the door opened again, and Darryl's head popped round the corner. 'Catch,' he said, throwing something gently towards her. 'Enjoy,' and he closed the door again.

Eleanor jumped at the intrusion but caught the miniature pot of jam that he must have pinched from the bar and ran back up the stairs with.

'Knife?' she asked the closed door.

15

Darryl enjoyed his day at work. The beautiful weather always made working outside a pleasure. The visitors were considerate and fascinated by the site. It was refreshing to talk to them and explain his work, and the significance of this particular mosaic he was unearthing. Ultimately, it was good to focus on something else for a while. Something other than his home on fire or his daughter dropping out of Uni.

He was about to get in the land rover for the journey home when his mobile sounded. A text from Alex.

Being hassled by K to let you know I'm fine. I'm fine xx

Darryl immediately called her, but her phone rang through to the answerphone. He texted back.

Thanks but would like a bit more. Just want to know why. Is there something I can do to help? Call me. xx

He paused over the send button before deleting the last 'xx' and typed

Please xx

If she's made this attempt at contact, surely, she must be open to revealing more. He sat waiting, absentmindedly tapping his phone against the steering wheel as he gazed across the fields in front of him. A hopeless wait. She wasn't going to call. After all, he should be grateful for the text. After ten minutes, he gave up and started the engine. At that moment, he forgot his pleasant day. During his twenty-minute journey back to the pub, his thoughts were now preoccupied with his daughter. Pulling into the pub car park, his phone rang.

'Hi, Dad.' Alex's voice was flat. He had heard that tone many times, especially during her early teenage years. The tone that said she was just waiting for an argument.

'Alex.' Darryl hadn't realised how worried he was about her until he heard her voice. He'd had so many questions for her, and now the moment was here his mind had gone blank.

'I just need some time, Dad. Please don't worry.'

'I'm afraid I do worry. It's a necessary part of the job. What's happened? Don't you like it at university?'

'It's not that exactly.'

'Then what?' Darryl hesitated before asking his next question. 'Boyfriend trouble?'

'Why does everything have to be about sex?'

Darryl flinched at Alex's aggressive tone. He tried to keep his voice calm. 'We're just worried that you...' He hesitated, choosing his words carefully.

'What Dad? Worried that I've made the same mistake as you and Mum did?'

'No, of course not. It's just that you have your entire future ahead of you and now is not a good time for having a...' Darryl drifted off. He couldn't bring himself to say it. 'That is, if you are... then we'll support you.'

'I'm not pregnant, Dad. There, are you happy?'

Darryl's tension eased. He had never thought of his two girls as a mistake and he wouldn't have changed a thing. But the pregnancy wasn't planned, and he and Rachel had been young. He understood that now.

'Well,' Alex continued after a brief silence. A little calmer, but still a hint of animosity in her voice. 'Now we have that all cleared up, am I allowed to live my life the way I want to?'

'Are you sure there isn't something I can help with? Even if it's just to talk over some options.'

'I know what my options are, I'm just waiting for—'

'For what?' He was getting closer.

'I've applied to change course,' Alex said bluntly.

'OK, is that all?' Darryl laughed with surprise. 'Why all the mystery?'

'I needed to audition and I'm waiting to hear whether I've got in. But I'm not going back to art history if I don't.'

'Audition? What's the course?'

'Drama.'

'As in acting? That's a tough life. A lot of travelling and that's if you can get the work in the first place.'

'Travelling never did you any harm.'

'Really? You have noticed that your mother and I got divorced?'

Alex was quiet.

'If that's what you want to do, sweetheart, then you do it. I can't say your mother will like it—'

'But it's not her life.' Alex was quick to answer. 'It's my life, and I want to be me.'

'What do you mean? You've always made certain everybody knows you're you.' Although identical, it hadn't been difficult to tell the difference between his two girls from an early age. And it was always Alex that people learnt first. Always Alex, who was found doing something that she shouldn't be. Always Alex wanting to stand out from the crowd.

'It's hard when... when you're a twin. I love Kathy, you know I do, but I just want to be me. I want to be Alex, not "one of the twins."'

'Of course you do, and if this is what you want, I'm not going to stop you.' He had never heard her sound so torn before. She and Kathy had always been different, but still the best of friends. He never thought there could ever be tension between them. 'When do you hear whether you've got a place?' he said, trying to turn the conversation more positive. He climbed out of the car and walked round to the pub entrance.

'Next week. Can I ask you to tell Mum?'

'Of course. You know, come to think of it, she may not take it as badly as you think. There was a time when she would dearly have loved to have done the same.'

'Mum?'

'Yes, Mum. She hasn't always just been your mother, you know.' The tension now broken, Darryl realised how much he missed his two girls. The odd text now and again was no replacement for seeing them, talking to them, wrapping his arms around them. 'I'd like to come and see you sometime. You can take me out for a meal as penance. And you haven't even met Eleanor yet.'

'Yeah, maybe during the holidays. We'll see.'

Darryl had heard that before. He knew it would be awhile yet before he got to see either of his girls again. There was always something more important to do than see their dad.

'I've got to go now, Dad,' she went on.

'Of course. Thanks for confiding in me. Just don't leave it so long next time. I'll see you soon. Love you.' He rang off as he turned to run up the stairs. At least that was one thing off his mind, although he didn't relish the idea of telling Rachel.

~

Eleanor's nerves wouldn't let her enjoy her day of quiet solitude. She bathed for over an hour, running through scenarios in her head about how she could start a conversation with Alison. Darryl was always so laid back, it was easy for him. Eleanor had always struggled with small talk. She attempted to visit the village shop several times, but seeing Shaun through the window, she had thought better of it and walked away again. How much would she be able to find out with him lingering around? Instead, she strolled out of the village and down pathways that led her through fields and round orchards. But, no matter what she did, the tranquil surroundings couldn't stop her from thinking of their house lying in ruins on the other side of a hill or two. Tempted to return to see how bad the damage was, she decided against it, afraid it may put her in the frame of mind of never wanting to go back there. Especially after spending a day and night in comparative luxury in their one room at the pub.

After lunch she had organised her clothes, ready for working at the school in the morning. Three times. With her nerves getting the better of her, she sat in the pub instead of the silence of her room. Unfortunately, for Eleanor, everyone she knew from the village, and even a few people she didn't, came into the pub at one time or another, and enquired how she was coping. Each time, she rallied her spirits and silently wished to be left alone. Her skin crawled at the sight of Shaun when he arrived. He sat at the bar, watching her, but never enquiring. This only served to put Eleanor more on edge.

One of the last to arrive had been Stella. She bought a takeaway coffee from the bar and sauntered over to Eleanor.

'I'm simply gasping for a coffee. I haven't stopped all day.' She brushed the seat on the bench next to her and made herself comfortable. 'How are you feeling now? Such a traumatic event to go through,' Stella drawled.

'OK, th—'

'I hope Carl finds out soon who is doing this to you.'

'We d—'

'He hasn't slept a wink for days with all this stress.'

Eleanor's shock prevented her from even trying to reply. She should have known better than to think Stella's compassion could have been for her.

'Where's Darryl today?'

'At wor—'

'Must be lonely on your—' Stella suddenly let out a yell as her coffee spilt across the table. The cup knocked over as she attempted to hitch her bag onto her shoulder.

'I'm so sorry. I'm so clumsy.' Stella grabbed a handful of serviettes from the container that Eleanor had moved to the edge of the table and mopped up the puddle that was spreading quickly across it.

Eleanor still had hold of the newspaper and had pulled it clear. Shaun left his stool at the bar, quick to join them. He brought more serviettes from the bar to help; the landlord, Tom, following close behind with a cloth. All the time, Stella flustered about, making the situation worse while they cleaned and dried the table.

'I'll get you another coffee, Stella,' Tom said, taking the pile of sodden serviettes with him.

His tone gave the impression that this wasn't the first time this had happened. Shaun took the opportunity to sit on the bench next to Eleanor, while Stella hesitantly perched on the edge of a stool opposite. She didn't make any argument about having her seat taken. In fact, she didn't make any hint of acknowledgement towards him. Shaun, relaxed and comfortable, seemed amused by the situation. He stared directly at

Stella as though welcoming an argument. Nervously, Stella began again with her questions.

'Did you sleep well? Is it nice here? I've often wondered whether I should recommend it to my clients. Sometimes they come from out of town and stay for a few days while they take in the area.'

Eleanor didn't attempt a reply as the landlord appeared with Stella's coffee and, quickly standing, she announced she was already late for a meeting with a client and had to leave.

'I'll tell you what, though,' she continued hurriedly, 'I'll pop round to the school at lunchtime tomorrow and see how you're getting on. A bit of moral support, that sort of thing.'

She pulled her phone from her pocket and left, frantically pressing buttons on the screen.

Eleanor didn't get the chance to tell that wouldn't be necessary and, though glad that Stella had left, she was now stuck with Shaun.

'She doesn't seem to like you very much,' Eleanor said, gripping onto the newspaper like a shield between them.

Shaun pulled a face as though to say he didn't care. 'It all goes back to our school days. I'm the only one who actually had the courage to tell her what an annoying bitch she is. I like to make my feelings clear.' He stretched his arm out, running it along the back of the bench, behind Eleanor's shoulders.

'I had noticed.' Eleanor fidgeted uncomfortably. She spread the paper on the table in front of her and shifted along the bench. Even just a few millimetres away was better than nothing.

'Please, continue,' Shaun said, gesturing towards the newspaper. 'I wouldn't want to interrupt.'

Eleanor stared at the paper, making a show of reading, but constantly aware of Shaun's intense stare.

'You know I saw you this morning,' Shaun said.

'I'm sorry.' Confused, Eleanor turned to look at Shaun.

'I saw you. This morning. How many times did you come over to the shop? One look at Alison and you walked away again.' He moved closer. 'You don't need to hide your feelings.'

'I'm not hiding anything,' Eleanor retorted. She suddenly realised how foolish she had been. 'I was just walking round the village, trying to learn more about the area.' The tension in Eleanor grew every second. She jumped nervously when his phone rang. He pulled it from his pocket and declined the call. Immediately, it rang a second time. Again, he declined the call.

'Don't you think you should get that?' Eleanor asked the third time the phone rang.

'It's nothing urgent,' he replied, giving Eleanor his full attention. 'There are more important things—'

'Shaun.' Alison stood over them. 'May I have your assistance at the shop, please? I need to go into town.'

Shaun stretched and slowly rose from the bench, while Alison turned to Eleanor with more of a grimace than a smile. 'Sorry to take my husband away from you.'

Eleanor was relieved by her appearance, though not her tone.

'Now's your chance,' Shaun whispered as he left.

The event had given Eleanor what she needed. A motive for Alison. She remembered the photograph in the tea-room, where Alison and Shaun were holding hands, although at the same time Jo had told them he had a thing for Miss Starling. Miss Starling disappeared soon after the photo had been taken. Maybe Alison saw Miss Starling as a threat. Wanting Shaun for herself, she thought with Miss Starling gone, there would be nothing in the way of their happily ever after. *Poor deluded woman.*

By the time Darryl arrived back from work, Eleanor had tucked herself away in a corner and was absorbed in an article that had followed the inquest of Fred Fletcher. The death at Black Spot Bridge that Stella had alluded to. Eleanor resorted to hiding behind the newspapers. She couldn't see who was in the pub, but neither could anybody see her. Shaun had left half an hour ago, and she was now reading the detailed account of how Black Spot Bridge had claimed many lives over the last couple of decades. The most recent being Fred Fletcher, and two weeks earlier, three young men who had drowned before they could make it out of the car. One of which had been the farmer's son and would have travelled along that road many times and knew the danger. Reading between the lines, the boys had a reputation for fast driving, and the result was tragic, but inevitable. Eleanor had often wondered why the farmer had always seemed so sad when they had seen him. Now she knew.

Absorbed in the article, she didn't notice Darryl arrive until she heard his voice as he walked straight past her to the stairs.

'I'll see you soon. Love you,' and he hung up. His footsteps trotted up the wooden stairs.

Eleanor felt as though her heart stopped. With everything they had been through together, they had a special bond. But he had never said those words to her. In fact, she had often been afraid of him saying them. But now, to know that he was saying them to someone else, she felt sick. She got up from her table and almost ran out of the pub. The newspaper slipping off the table behind her and onto the floor. She walked and kept on walking, with no thoughts as to where.

~

Darryl swung open the door to their room, a spring in his step. Relief had swept through him after his talk with Alex.

'Eleanor,' he called.

He stuck his head through the door to the bathroom in his

search. He jogged back down the stairs and looked around the bar on his way back through.

'Have you seen Eleanor?' he asked the landlord serving behind the bar.

'She left straight after you came in,' he said. 'I have to say, she didn't look too happy.'

Darryl sped up as he left the pub and looked around him. It only took a moment before he saw her walking along the road that led to the primary route to Northwood gate.

'Eleanor!' he called, but she didn't hear him.

He crossed the lane to the green, his steps quickening with concern. Her head down; her march determined. Something was wrong. Watching for traffic, he kept a cursory eye on a dark red car that pulled off from the side of the road, a little ahead of him, not wanting to cross its path if it turned his way. But his primary focus was on Eleanor. He couldn't understand where she would be going.

∼

The sound of an engine crept into Eleanor's mind and she moved subconsciously to the side of the road, but kept walking. A habit evolving from walking down the narrow country lanes. Oblivious to the scorching sun on her back. A silent void in her head. Darryl called after her, again and again, but she forced it from her mind. She couldn't speak to him now. She needed time and space.

∼

Darryl, almost across the green, slowed as the red car had turned the sharp bend round the corner of the village green. A large ornamental hedge had blocked it from view for a moment, but it would cross his path, and he hesitantly hung back. Suddenly, there was the sound of screeching tyres. Black smoke rose into the air.

'Eleanor!' Darryl screamed.

∽

The sound of the car suddenly became louder, forcing itself into Eleanor's consciousness. Tyres screeched, and the engine roared. She heard Darryl call again, louder, but it wasn't just a call. More like a warning. She turned and saw the car. So close to her, its distorted size was more reminiscent of a tank than the small hatchback it was. She was already on the verge of the road. With nowhere left to go, she only had one choice. Without thinking, she leaped into the bushes that created the boundary between the road and a field full of wheat. The front corner of the car clipped her ankle as she dived through the air, spinning her sideways.

In a moment Darryl was at her side.

'Are you alright? Are you hurt?' he asked impatiently.

'I'm fine,' she retorted.

'That was deliberate,' Darryl said, pulling her from the bush and holding her tight. 'Somebody doesn't like you snooping. I'm beginning to think that maybe there's something in your crazy theories after all.'

16

Eleanor struggled to free herself from Darryl's grasp. His touch repulsed her. She pushed herself away from him, but cried out in pain when she tried to put weight on her left foot.

'Lean on me. It's going to be fine.' Darryl reached for Eleanor again. 'I've got the number plate. We can get the car traced.'

The car hadn't stopped. It had screeched along the road and was soon out of sight.

'Who is she?' Eleanor forced through gritted teeth, pushing him away again.

'Was it a woman driving? Did you see?' Darryl asked. His words falling over themselves in his agitation.

'Who is she?' Eleanor repeated louder. 'If there's someone else, just tell me. I just want to know. I can't stand being in this constant limbo.'

She turned to face him, only to be confronted by a puzzled expression. 'The woman in the cafe,' she continued defiantly. 'Don't try to deny it. The beautiful, dark-haired woman in the cafe. Who is she?'

'You know about her?' Darryl asked, his brow raising with surprise.

'Yes, I know about her. I saw you together and you've said nothing.'

'I haven't exactly had the opportunity. She turned up at work on Friday and it's been murders and mayhem ever since. I didn't want to give you anything else to be worrying about.'

'So, it *is* something for me to worry about.' Eleanor had her answer. She started towards the pub, but her ankle slowed her down.

Darryl grabbed her arm as she passed him. 'No, you don't need to worry about her. That was Rachel.'

'Your ex-wife Rachel? But I heard you on the phone telling her you love her.'

'I haven't told her I loved her for years,' Darryl insisted.

'I heard you on the phone. Just now when you arrived at the pub. You told her you I—'

Darryl laughed loudly. That broad laugh she had grown so fond of now infuriated her.

'I was talking to Alex. My daughter,' he clarified.

Eleanor, stunned and still standing in the middle of the road, couldn't move. Darryl helped her to a nearby bench and explained.

'Rachel turned up because I wasn't answering her calls. She wanted to let me know that Alex is dropping out of Uni. At that time, we didn't know why, or even where she was living, other than staying with a friend. With everything else that's been going on, I didn't want you to be worrying about this, too.'

Eleanor's mind whirled with information that she had never considered.

'I'm sorry,' Darryl continued. 'There were times I tried to tell you, but other things kept cropping up. And I'm afraid you're never going to stop me from telling my kids I love them, but that doesn't mean I love you any less.'

Eleanor looked up into his face.

'Do you?' she asked. Afraid of hearing it for all these months, now she realised she craved it.

'What? Love you? Well, I may have to think about it for a while,' he teased. 'Yes, I do,' he replied seriously.

'Everything happened so quickly between us,' Eleanor said. 'It took the thought of losing you to another woman to realise it, but I think I love you, too.'

'I can't believe you knew about Rachel all this time.' Darryl shook his head and laughed. 'Why didn't you tell me?'

'Why didn't *you* tell *me*?'

'I was trying to protect you.' Darryl smiled and moved to kiss her.

'So,' Eleanor interrupted. 'Why is Alex dropping out of Uni?'

'She's not so much dropping out as moving to another course. Apparently, she's decided she wants to be a film star.'

'A film star? Is that what she said?'

'Not exactly, but that's what it means.'

Eleanor smiled at him, examining his face. She never wanted to hate that face again.

'No more secrets, please?' she implored.

'No more secrets.'

∾

On their way back to the pub, doors were closing around the village green. The noise of the screeching car had pulled people out of their houses, stopping to watch the pantomime in front of them. At first she cringed with embarrassment, but then looking around at the buildings, Eleanor couldn't help but wonder how many secrets hid behind those doors. For a body to be hidden for twenty years and yet somehow nobody missed her, it didn't seem possible. Did nobody search for her? What else were they hiding?

Darryl, having managed to get the licence plate number, kept repeating it over and over, ingraining it into his memory until Carl arrived half an hour after Darryl's call. The paramedics had already attended and Eleanor now sat on the same bench she had spent most of her afternoon on, with her leg rested along the bench itself. Her ankle lifted onto a tapestry patchwork cushion that matched the rest of the decor in the pub, a cold compress on her ankle, and a crocheted blanket wrapped around her shoulders. She had watched Darryl as he nervously switched his attention between fussing over her and pacing a two-metre length of the bar while he had been waiting.

'Are you sure this wasn't just an accident?' Carl asked tentatively.

'I'm certain. I saw the whole thing,' Darryl said forcefully. 'The car pulled out and followed her. It turned the corner onto her road and sped up so fast that - in fact, come out and see the skid marks on the road where it sped up so fast.' Darryl headed for the front door, pleading for the DCI to follow.

He waved his hand gently to motion that wasn't necessary. Both Eleanor and Darryl already knew that others more specialised in that area were attending to the scene, and so Darryl returned and continued his account.

'I could see that Eleanor had heard the car. She moved over to the side, like any normal person would, but then it swerved. It *swerved* to hit her. If I hadn't called her, got her attention, she wouldn't have turned to see it and this would be a very different situation right now.' Darryl's frustration was turning into anger. 'In fact, I bet it was waiting. It was waiting outside by the green. Waiting for Eleanor. And you think this could have been an accident? More like attempted murder. Have you found the car yet?'

'It's been less than an hour since you provided us with the licence plate and description. I like to think of myself as efficient,

Mr Westwood, but I'm not a miracle worker,' the DCI said calmly.

Eleanor squirmed at Darryl's persistence. She just wanted the whole situation to disappear.

'What about CCTV from the shop?' Darryl continued. 'Or does anywhere else have it? You may be able to see their face.'

'CCTV?' Carl asked, quietly amused. 'In Bramblemere? Nothing happens here to warrant the use of CCTV.'

'Nothing happens here?' Darryl repeated sarcastically. 'We found a body in our garden, someone set light to our house, and now attempted murder?'

'Nothing has happened here until you arrived,' DCI Hanson corrected himself.

'So, it's our fault?'

'That's not what I'm saying, Mr Westwood.'

'Darryl,' Eleanor interrupted before he could say any more. 'Calm down. I'm fine. They'll catch whoever it was from the description you gave, and we'll all live happily ever after.' It impressed her how Carl stayed calm with Darryl's abuse flying at him.

Darryl looked at her sternly.

'Please,' she implored. She didn't want any more fuss. She pulled the blanket tighter round her shoulders, cold with tiredness.

'I would suggest you stay here in the pub for now until we can get this whole business wrapped up, or until we can make other arrangements,' the DCI said, raising from his seat and leaving to speak quietly with Tom behind the bar.

After the DCI and the paramedics had left the pub, and after Eleanor and Darryl had eaten, Eleanor could put a small amount of weight on her foot again. The swelling had reduced, but the ankle still ached. Nonetheless, Eleanor was able to hobble her way up the stairs to their room without Darryl's help, where they argued for most of the evening. Darryl didn't want her going to work at the school tomorrow. But Eleanor's determination was as strong as ever. The shock from the afternoon's event was passing and her mind was clearing.

'Carl was quite clear that he didn't want us wandering off.'

'I'm not wandering off, and anyway, I'm sure it was a suggestion, not an order. And nobody's going to try anything at the school,' she said, exasperated at his persistence.

'It depends how desperate they are, and let's face it, they must be desperate to try and run you down in broad daylight.'

Eleanor wished Darryl wouldn't say things like that. "Run her down," "attempted murder." It made it all too real. She had somehow separated herself from the event, and if it wasn't for the sore ankle, she could almost have believed it had happened to somebody else.

'If someone is actually trying to kill me,' she forced herself to say the words, 'then surely it's better we find out sooner rather than later who it is. As you said, we did well last time.'

'As you said, more by luck than judgement.'

∼

Eleanor woke the following morning with a heavy combination of determination and trepidation. It still infuriated Darryl that she insisted on going to work at the school, but her stubbornness grew with every protest.

'I'll walk you to the school,' Darryl said as Eleanor finished tying her hair back into a smart ponytail.

'It's two minutes away,' she said, snatching at her handbag, ready to leave.

'And a car hit you less than two minutes away.' He paused and reined in his temper. 'I'm walking you there. You can at least let me do that.'

They left the pub in silence and walked towards the school where children were already arriving. Eleanor faltered as she neared. Children were running and screaming round the playground. Holding on to their mother's hands while they waited. Eleanor clenched her fist at the memory of holding her own son's tiny hand before catching the look on Darryl's face.

'Are you sure you want to do this?' he asked.

'Yes,' she said. Her face as austere as her voice.

'I didn't mean... I just meant... The kids. I know it's going to be har—'

'I'm doing it.' Eleanor left without another word.

She left Darryl behind, watching her as she dodged between the cars that had filled the usually empty lane. From across the road, he watched Becky greet her at the gate and consoled himself with the fact that at least nothing was likely to happen inside the school. He looked around at the parents. Some hardly got out of their car before sending off their children, presumably before rushing off to work. Others waited, gazing after them till the last moment when they disappeared through the large central door. And a couple of small groups of three or four parents hung around chatting, with no intention of leaving anytime soon.

This was a side of parenthood Darryl had hardly ever experienced. Away from family life for so much of the time, Rachel had the job of the school run. His job involved searching for the pieces of other people's lives, to understand how people had lived hundreds of years ago. And now, the irony struck him how he had been so focused on learning about those other people's lives that he had missed so much of his own family's.

The screech of a car's tyres brought Darryl's thoughts back to the present. His first thoughts were of Eleanor. He quickly found her, still in the playground with Becky. Angry voices came from the same direction as the screech. A child had stepped into the road, or was it a parent too keen to leave? The incident left Darryl wondering if anybody there could be responsible for Eleanor's hit-and-run yesterday. Everybody seemed so normal. How would he be able to tell what a killer looked like? Then he saw Shaun. He was watching from a short distance away on the village green. Darryl turned in time to see Eleanor disappear through the open doors and into the school building, before turning back to Shaun. But he was gone. Looking around, Darryl saw him hurrying towards the shop, where Alison stood at the doorway. *Please, let it be him,* Darryl thought.

The cars that had lined the lane disappeared as quickly as they had arrived. Even the chatting parents strolled away towards the small housing estate on the edge of the village, leaving Darryl standing on his own at the edge of the green. Out of habit, he checked his phone for a message, but there was none. After texting Alex earlier for an update, he knew it would be too soon for a reply, but he had to try. Sensing an ominous silence around him, his senses heightened by the events of yesterday, he jogged back to the pub. On returning to their room, he noticed Eleanor had left her lunch behind. Sandwiches made by the pub kitchens were still sitting on the side cabinet. Pleased at the excuse to go back to the school, he decided to wait until lunchtime, hoping the morning would give her the chance to calm down.

His phone rang. He took it out of his pocket, eager to speak to Alex again, but saw the name Rachel. Having not yet spoken to her after his first conversation with Alex, he tossed the ringing phone onto the bedside cabinet. He'd already had one hostile conversation this morning, he didn't fancy another.

∼

Eleanor had struggled all morning. The prospect of being so close to children, especially around the same age as Chris when he died, was overwhelming. But also, Darryl had been suffocating her all morning. She understood his need to try to protect her, but her patience was wearing thin. Frustrated with him, she was glad to be walking away, though not enthralled with where she was heading.

Becky had welcomed her as an old friend, as Eleanor knew she would. After spending some time greeting the children as they arrived, Becky then directed her to Susan to sign a couple of forms before she could start in the classroom. Eleanor, determined to focus on her key priority for being there, was grateful for the opportunity to speak with the secretary.

Susan was chatting with a mother through the open hatch window when Eleanor entered the reception area. The parent rocked a pushchair back and forth where a grumpy toddler sat while his mother chatted about the state of affairs at home. After several minutes of waiting with nothing more than a nod of acknowledgement from Susan, the grumpy boy let out a tremendous wail. Eleanor presumed he must have been as bored as she was. The rocking became harder as the mother attempted to continue her conversation, changing the subject to the annoyance of screaming kids.

'But maybe that's not a conversation for here and now,' Susan said cheerfully.

The mother begrudgingly agreed, said her goodbyes and turned her attention to her son. Susan's smile dropped as soon as the mother and her wailing child left the building. 'She drives me crazy, that woman,' Susan said with a vast sigh. 'I swear they think I have nothing better to do than listen to their tales of woe.'

Eleanor laughed with surprise. Susan had looked as though she was interested and even enjoying the gossip, though now

Eleanor thought about it she realised it had been a very one-sided conversation.

'Come on into the office, dear,' Susan continued, peering over the top of her glasses that were perched on the end of her nose. 'There are a couple of things you need to sign and then I'll take you down to the classroom.'

Eleanor walked through to the office. On the wall surrounding the hatch were family photographs and crudely made paintings. Not visible from the reception, but from the office side, Eleanor's eyes couldn't help but be drawn to the colourful display.

'That's my family,' Susan said. 'And these are my grandchildren, Poppy, Simon and Robyn. Robyn's the artistic one. These are all her paintings. The other two won't stay still long enough.'

'You certainly look as though you've settled in. How long have you worked here?'

'It must be over forty years now,' Susan said with another tremendous sigh. 'I can't leave. I don't know how to do anything else. Retirement looms in just a few years anyway, but I have a feeling it would be less work staying on here than being at home with the grandchildren. I love them dearly, but it's always a relief to hand them back.' She laughed jovially, her glasses almost slipping off the end of her nose.

Eleanor was relieved how easily Susan had begun chatting. Like most grandmothers, she clearly doted on her grandchildren.

'They look like they could be a handful.' Eleanor made a point of looking closely at the family gathering while Susan beamed with pride.

'Forty years,' Eleanor went on. 'You must have seen a lot of people come and go.'

'Many, many people come and go.'

'Though none quite so tragically as Miss Starling,' Eleanor added jokingly.

'But maybe that's not a conversation for here and now,' Susan said after a stilted pause. She turned away abruptly and picked up several sheets of paper from her desk. Handing them to Eleanor with a pen, she said, 'You'd better read through them first. Just let me know when you're done.'

Susan presented Eleanor with the back of her head as she sat and span on her chair, returning to her computer. Remembering Susan had ended the previous conversation with the mother with the exact same phrase left Eleanor intrigued. Could it mean that Susan had something to tell but didn't want to discuss it here, or had Eleanor been snubbed? Concerned she had lost her opportunity to find out more, she concluded it was a problem she could deal with later. At least she had discovered that it was a topic Susan wasn't comfortable in discussing, and that in itself was interesting. The question was, why? She needed more thought on how to manage Susan.

On completion of the forms, Susan returned to her jovial self and led Eleanor to the classroom. Even though she was friendly, Eleanor still had the feeling that Susan wanted her out of her office as quickly as possible. Becky, though, visibly relaxed as Eleanor arrived, and was much more welcoming. Becky introduced Eleanor to the class where, after her worries that morning, she found the children were a welcome distraction. For the first couple of hours. Soon, the noise, the mess, and the clothes pulling were all too much, and she fought not to snap at them. The children were fun. There was no denying that. They laughed and played. There seemed no end to their enthusiasm. But as time went on, Eleanor found it more and more difficult to shake the expectation of seeing Chris's face looking up at her. Each time a child pulled on her trouser leg, she looked down with anticipation, but only felt disappointment. Each time a small hand reached for hers, she held it tight, but her heart sank a little further, knowing that it wasn't the hand she wanted to hold. It wasn't long before she found herself whirling with overwhelming thoughts of those she had lost. Her love for them had only brought her pain.

Relief finally came a short while before lunch. Becky's hand appeared on her shoulder.

'Why don't you go to the staff-room and make us coffees?' Her voice was soft and comforting. 'Get the coffees in early, then we can make full use of the quiet at lunchtime.'

Eleanor realised Becky must have guessed something was wrong, no matter how much she tried to hide it. Grateful for the respite, Eleanor disappeared to the staff-room and took advantage of the time to compose herself. Rinsing her face in cold water and snatching at her breaths till they became easier. How did she ever think this would be a good idea? In the quiet of the staff-room, she could steady herself and bring her focus back to why she was there. If she was going to make herself go through all this, she needed to make it worth her while. She took the opportunity to examine the patio and her spirits rose with the realisation that she had been right; they were the same honey-coloured slabs as the ones she had been lifting in her garden the day she had discovered Jennifer Nightingale. Poor Jennifer Nightingale. A lifetime of running and hiding, only for it to end with a traumatic death. Eleanor's nerves were already in tatters. It didn't take much for a vision of Jenny to force its way into her head, fighting for her life beneath the patio slabs. Pushing the palms of her hands against her eyes, Eleanor backed away. 'Focus, focus,' she reprimanded herself. Wiping the tears from her eyes, Eleanor returned to the kettle and finished making the coffees.

Becky was dismissing the children for lunch as she arrived back at the classroom. She hesitated at the doorway, watching the children run out of the class through a door that led directly onto the playground. A crescendo of noise followed them.

'Are you alright?' Becky asked, taking her coffee from Eleanor and perching on the edge of her desk.

'I'm sorry. The last thing you need is an emotional wreck in the room with you.' Eleanor had wiped her eyes, but they still pricked with redness.

'Don't be silly. You've been through a lot over the last few days. To be honest, it surprised me to see you here at all after what's happened.'

Eleanor was relieved Becky had assumed that her distress was because of recent events. They'd had a brief discussion earlier about the fire at the house, but there was no time for great detail, especially with young children around. And Eleanor didn't want to bring up the close call she'd had yesterday.

'Is there anything I can do to help?' Becky continued. 'You really don't need to be here; maybe you should take the day for yourself. I can cope.'

'No,' she shook her head, trying to wipe more tears that were forcing their way through. 'I think it's better if I keep going. Actually, I was just thinking about Miss Starling while I was in the staff-room. Being here, where she worked, it seems to make her more real somehow.'

'Yes, I can see that,' Becky said.

She sipped at her coffee and watched the ripples as she blew on the hot liquid. Clearly uncomfortable with talking about Miss Starling, but Eleanor persevered. It was why she was there, after all, and the quicker she could get some worthwhile information, the better.

'We met her sister on Friday. Actually, she was sitting on our doorstep when we got home after seeing you and Will. She told us that Miss Starling was hiding from an abusive husband and had become terrified of all men. In fact, that's why she struggled to have any kind of interaction with adults. He had abused her both mentally and physically.'

'That's awful,' Becky whispered. Her posture stiffened with discomfort.

Becky clenched one hand into a fist. It was clear she didn't want to hear this, but there was information Eleanor needed and only Becky could provide it.

'So, there wouldn't have been any boyfriend. What made you think there was?'

'I — I can only tell you what she said. She said she had a boyfriend, and he was going to be joining her soon.' Becky's hands trembled as she gripped her mug. Her cheeks burned red, her eyes unable to leave her coffee.

She was clearly distraught from these questions, but Eleanor needed answers. Her heart ached for Becky, and she hesitated, wondering whether she should continue. But now, someone was targeting her. This was no longer a tragedy from twenty years ago, but a very real and present danger. And so she continued.

'Her sister's devastated, as I'm sure you can imagine, having spent the last twenty-odd years searching for her. She wanted to see where Miss Starling had been buried all this time and, when I took her, I noticed the patio slabs that had hidden her body look exactly like the ones on the patio by the French doors in the staff-r—'

'Those slabs are very popular,' Becky interrupted. 'They're everywhere.'

Eleanor caught a slight catch in her voice, and unfortunately for Becky, Eleanor persisted.

'You would have been working here when they laid the patio. Do you know if it was meant to be bigger?'

Becky scrunched her eyes closed tight. Tears ran down her cheeks. Eleanor gave in. She couldn't do this anymore. This poor woman, distraught at Eleanor's making after her kindness and generosity. Eleanor put down her mug and crossed to Becky. Placing an arm around her shoulder, she perched on the edge of the table next to her. She opened her mouth, ready to say some comforting words and apologise for causing so much distress. But before she had the chance to say anything, Becky's hands slipped from her coffee mug as she gave a silent scream. She crumpled before Eleanor's eyes as her mug fell in slow motion to the floor. Eleanor floundered, not knowing what to do.

'I'm sorry,' she said. 'I'm so sorry.' Her words felt inadequate for what she had done.

'You know, don't you?' Becky whispered. 'I always knew it would come to this one day.'

'Look who I found delivering somebody's lunch,' came a deep voice entering through the doorway behind them.

Eleanor turned and saw Will and Darryl standing open-mouthed, staring at the two women. Stunned, she couldn't move.

'I did it,' Becky whispered. 'I did it, I did it,' each time louder until she shouted, 'I did it.'

17

Becky took a deep breath, her shoulders juddering as the air filled her lungs. She opened her eyes and looked around her, stopping at the astonished look on her husband's face.

'I did it,' she said quietly and calmly. 'I hit her on the back of the head with one of the slabs. She caught me stealing them. The school was closed for the weekend, but she had come in to collect some work she'd forgotten to take home. I startled her. She didn't expect to see me, and she dropped her books. As she bent over to pick them up, the slab slipped. I never have been very strong, and they were heavy. I couldn't hold it any longer. It slipped and hit...' Her words drifted off. Unable to finish the sentence. 'It was an accident. I didn't mean to kill her.'

'There never was a boyfriend, was there?' Eleanor asked, dazed by Becky's confession.

'No, I made it up. She was such a recluse, living out there all on her own. Nobody else ever really knew her. It was easy to do.'

'Rebecca, what are you saying?' Will's face was pale. He stumbled slightly, as though his legs wouldn't hold him.

Becky covered her face with her hands and wept.

'I can't believe it,' Will said. 'I won't believe it. She can't have done,' he implored towards Eleanor as though she was judge and jury. 'She works tirelessly for the village. A wonderful mother. A wonderful wife. Never asking for anything for herself. She epitomises the pillar of the community spirit.' His voice faded as his pillar crumbled in front of him.

'I never asked for anything because I don't deserve anything. I have lived with the guilt of what I have done for the last twenty years.' Becky said in a thick, strangled voice. 'I couldn't let her death be for nothing. Every time I thought of myself, I remembered what I had taken and tried to do some good with the life that was left behind. My life. I've always known this day would come, and now I'm glad it's over. Now I can breathe.'

Eleanor's mind was in turmoil. Somehow, she had got Becky to confess. There should have been relief. Justice for Jennifer. Then why did she feel numb? She stood and watched as Becky collapsed to the floor. Paralysed by her confusion.

Darryl and Will rushed forward to help, but Will turned on Darryl, stopping him from getting anywhere near his wife.

'I think you had better leave. Both of you,' he growled. He now stood tall and straight; a pretence of strength, while his wife sat crumpled on the floor, quietly sobbing. Turning directly to Eleanor, he said, 'I'm afraid your services aren't required for the rest of the day, or for the foreseeable future. I will ask Susan to contact all the parents to come and collect their children. Please leave the premises. Now.'

An uncomfortable silence filled the room. Even the sound of children playing outside didn't register in Eleanor's ears. They left the room, leaving Will to tend to his wife.

In a daze, Eleanor and Darryl walked back towards the reception area and out through the main door. Once outside the school, they drifted towards the pub. Darryl finally broke the silence.

'I asked you to find out where she used to live, not to accuse her,' he said with a half-hearted attempt at sarcasm. 'Even so, well done.'

Eleanor stared straight ahead of her. Her eyes unable to focus.

'I brought you your lunch,' he said after another moment's pause. 'Eleanor, are you OK?'

'Can we stay out here for a while? I need the fresh air,' she said, almost overcome with a sudden rush of nausea.

They headed for a nearby bench overlooking the pond.

'I don't understand,' Eleanor whispered, still numb with shock and landing heavily on the bench.

'What? What is there to understand? You got her to confess to murder.' Darryl gently took hold of her hands.

'No. No, I didn't. I was just talking about Miss Starling, and the patio, and - next thing I know, she's collapsing in front of me. I didn't do it.' Eleanor shook her head. This wasn't right. She pulled away from Darryl, not knowing which way to look.

'It doesn't matter. She confessed. That's what's important. You caught the killer.'

Darryl's light-hearted laugh grated on Eleanor's nerves. 'But I don't want it to be Becky,' she blurted. 'I like Becky. It can't be her.' Tears welled in her eyes.

'I like Becky too,' Darryl said. 'But the fact remains, she confessed. Sounds like it was an accident, but then she covered it up, and that's not good. No matter how much you might like her, she made a mistake. A big one. But that's not your fault.'

'Can we go home now? Or at least back to the pub,' Eleanor added, thinking about the fire. Had that been Becky too? The idea seemed impossible. She looked up, turning her head towards the pub in anticipation of her move. Stella was trotting along the road, heading straight towards them from the pub car park. 'Oh no. I forgot about Stella,' she said. She didn't feel like talking to anyone, let alone Stella.

'What about her?' Darryl asked.

'She said she'd come and give some moral support during my lunch break.'

'Here, as promised,' Stella called as she approached. 'I don't like letting down a friend. Don't tell me you're trying to escape already? Oh my word, are you alright? You look very pale.'

Eleanor found she couldn't speak.

Luckily, Darryl took the lead instead. 'Had a bit of a shock.'

'What's happened? Anything I can do to help?' Stella asked, taking hold of Eleanor's hands.

'Not really,' Darryl said, hesitantly.

'Becky has just confessed to killing Miss Starling.' Eleanor stated the fact as pragmatically as she could, as if that would help make it seem possible, let alone true.

'Wh — Oh — Bec — No.' Stella's face paled, even under all her makeup. She staggered slightly and joined Eleanor and Darryl on the bench.

'No, you must have heard it wrong. Becky wouldn't do that.'

'I'm afraid there was no mistake.' Eleanor found her voice, annoyed by Stella's superior attitude.

'And she's been hiding it all these years?'

'She said it was an accide—' Eleanor tried to explain.

'Ha, an accident?'

'I don't believe she—' Eleanor tried again.

'Oh, don't you? It's not an accident if you hit twice.'

'What do you mean, hit twice?' Eleanor could hardly say the words.

'I'm sorry, I've said too much as it is. Blame the shock. She's one of my oldest friends, you know.'

'Do you mean someone hit Miss Starling twice?' Darryl persevered.

Stella hesitated. 'There have been a few developments, as my husband would call them. I'm sure Carl won't mind me telling you. It's not as if they could consider you suspects. Well, I guess nobody's a suspect now, if what you say is true.'

'What developments?' Eleanor interjected.

Stella looked around her and seeing no one else around, she leaned in and whispered. 'I guess you're going to find out soon enough anyway, but you didn't hear this from me.' She made another quick glance around before continuing. 'They have found two more bodies in the house.'

'In our house?' Eleanor exclaimed.

'Under the floorboards or something. Obviously, I don't know the details. I've told Carl I don't want to know about his cases, but when they are so close to home, it's difficult for him to hide them from me, and sometimes he needs a loving soul to share his troubles with.' Stella's self-righteous tone had returned, as though she was the only person in the world her beloved husband could depend on. 'Now, I've said too much already. This mouth of mine is going to get me into so much trouble. And now I come to think about it, I've always had the feeling Becky was too good to be true.'

'I'm sure there's a simple explanation. If we could find out what really happened and speak to her—'

'Oh no, no, no. We can't do that. Carl wouldn't like that at all. The best thing is to stay out of it and leave it to the police. There would be no point in speaking to her, anyway. She's obviously a liar and has had us all fooled for years.' Stella took some gasping breaths and stood. 'I need a stiff drink. Anybody joining me?'

'No, thank you,' both Eleanor and Darryl were keen to answer. 'I think I'd rather have the fresh air,' Eleanor continued.

Both were relieved to see Stella walking back towards the pub. They leaned back on the bench and breathed deep sighs of relief. Darryl thought Eleanor looked as pale as he felt. Two more bodies in the house.

'I don't believe it,' Eleanor said flatly.

'I know,' Darryl agreed. 'I can't believe this is happening.'

'I knew something wasn't right. Becky is not a killer,' Eleanor continued.

Darryl turned to look at Eleanor in amazement. 'She confessed,' Darryl said emphatically. 'Can we focus on the fact that there were bodies found in our house?'

'We can't help them, but we might be able to help Becky.'

Darryl didn't know what to say. She was right, but it would have been nice to have taken just a moment for some self pity.

After a pause Eleanor continued, 'Becky confessed to an accident and covering it up. She didn't confess to killing two more, let alone the second blow. She didn't do it.'

'I have to admit,' Darryl said thoughtfully, 'I had been wondering about how she could have moved Jenny.'

'I suppose in whatever vehicle she was using to steal the slabs.'

'But that's just it. She doesn't drive. Don't you remember? Will said Friday evening, she doesn't drive.'

Eleanor suddenly jumped. 'My bag. I must have left it in the classroom.'

'Do you think it's safe to go back in and get it yet?' Darryl didn't want another confrontation. He thought Will was going to hit him last time.

'I can't function without my bag. It has everything in it.'

Darryl looked suspiciously at Eleanor. 'And it could just be a good excuse for you to get to talk to Becky?'

'Maybe. If the opportunity arises.'

'Eleanor!'

'I need my bag.' Eleanor exclaimed. 'And - and I need to help Becky if I can.'

'Come on,' Darryl reluctantly agreed. 'Let's go while it's quiet, before everyone arrives to collect their children.'

18

Eleanor marched back to the school and entered. Darryl sauntered behind. The secretary, Susan, was busy on the phone and looking harassed. She glanced up to see who had entered, but turned away again quickly when she saw it was Eleanor. So, she waited patiently. Susan finished her call and opened the window hatch between them. Her eyes were red from crying, and she said nothing to greet Eleanor.

'I'm sorry to disturb you, but I've left my bag in the classroom.'

The phone rang, and Susan rolled her eyes.

'The news is out,' Susan said. She hesitated before letting Eleanor through the locked door that led through to the classrooms. 'and now I can't keep up with irate parents. You'd better go get it yourself. I guess it's not possible for you to do any more damage.'

Passing Will's office, Eleanor quickly glanced through the narrow window in the door. Becky and Will were alone, quietly waiting. Will stood, his hands clasped behind his back, gazing vacantly out of the window. Becky sat hunched, her eyes red and puffy. A pile of wet, crumpled tissues in her lap. Both avoiding the other's eyes.

The classroom itself was eerily quiet after the morning's activity. The remnants of play laid scattered in various areas of the room. Her skin crawling from the memories of everything that had happened there that morning, Eleanor quickly retrieved her bag and left again. Heading back towards the reception, Eleanor saw the door to Will's office open.

'A nice cup of tea while we wait. That's what we need,' came Will's voice.

The solution to everything. A nice cup of tea. Eleanor hung back and kept out of sight the best she could. Her heart thumped as she watched Will leave his office and head down the corridor that led to the staff-room. This could be her chance. The police haven't yet arrived, but it won't be long. At best, she only had the time it took to boil a kettle. Eleanor quietly slipped in through the door. Becky's head hung forward as though she didn't have the energy to lift it, but she jolted up at the sound of Eleanor's voice.

'I'm so sorry, Becky. I didn't mean for this to happen.'

Becky's eyes were bloodshot and puffy from crying. Her face was pale, her hair stuck to the sides of her face with her tears. She didn't say a word; she showed no sign of emotion. Eleanor recognised the same posture of numbness she had experienced herself so many times.

'I don't believe you did this,' Eleanor persevered.

'I told you what happened, and this is how it should be,' Becky said, resolved. 'I've lived with the secret for too long. It was suffocating me, and now I can breathe.'

Eleanor quickly glanced through the window. She knew she didn't have much time.

'I believe you were there, but someone else was there too, weren't they?' she asked gently.

Becky immediately began to shake her head.

'Who was it? Who was with you?'

Becky looked sternly at her. 'Nobody.'

'You got the body from the school to Rushmere cottage by yourself?' Eleanor asked.

'Yes,' she said firmly. 'I'm not saying it wasn't difficult, but I did it and you can't prove otherwise.'

Her face was stern. Her answer almost rehearsed, as though she was expecting the question.

'What about the other bodies?' Eleanor asked, watching Becky's expression closely. Her eyes darted across the room. She faltered for a moment before answering.

'What about them?' she asked.

'Did you kill them too?'

'Yes,' she replied firmly.

'All of them?'

'Yes,' she said, losing her patience.

'I guess burying them in the garden too was the obvious thing to do.'

'Yes, yes, yes,' Becky growled at her.

'Who were they?' Eleanor persevered.

'Nobodies. Just people who were in my way. They had found me out and were going to report me.'

'Who are you protecting?' Eleanor said. Her voice soft. 'You couldn't have done this on your own.'

'I did it. I did all of it. Now leave me alone.' Leaning forward, she buried her face in her lap and wept.

Eleanor glanced through the window again. Still no sign of Will. She had one last try.

'You didn't kill those others either,' she went on. 'They were buried in the house, not the garden.'

Becky didn't respond.

'Did you know she was hit twice?'

The soft sound of her crying stopped abruptly, and she looked back at Eleanor. Her face was wet with tears.

'I'm guessing you didn't.'

'We could have saved her,' Becky whispered so quietly Eleanor almost missed it.

'We?' Eleanor repeated softly, trying not to antagonise her, though her heart was racing.

But Becky only stared at her.

'You could have saved her,' Eleanor continued. 'Whoever you were with, hit her again. It wasn't you, Becky. Who was it?'

Becky only shook her head.

'You didn't do this. Whoever you're covering for has left you all these years believing you had murdered somebody.'

'No, he wouldn't.'

'Who wouldn't?' Eleanor asked.

Only silence followed. A silent scream as Becky clawed at her throat.

'Was it your boyfriend?'

Becky nodded reluctantly.

'Will said you had a nasty breakup with your boyfriend. Is this why? You broke up because of what happened with Miss Starling? What was his name?' asked Eleanor. The softness of her voice was full of empathy.

Becky suddenly shook her head, her eyes darting round the room.

'He left the village,' she rasped. 'Soon after, he left the village. He wanted me to go with him, but I couldn't leave Mum. So, he left and I've never seen him again.'

'But if you give us his name, the police can find him and it will help your plea,' Eleanor went on. 'You are not a murderer.'

Becky stood, resolute, and stared back at Eleanor. She shook her head.

'No,' she said firmly. 'I did it and I'm the one who should be punished.'

'What are you doing?' Will's shout came through the door. Before he had even opened it, he had seen Eleanor through the window.

She jumped at his booming voice. She had been so distracted she had forgotten to watch for him returning from the staff-room.

'Please, tell them his name. You didn't do this,' Eleanor implored as Will burst into the room. The drinks sloping over the edge of the mugs in his haste.

'Have you not caused enough trouble? Get out.'

'Think of your children,' Eleanor implored. 'Think of what it will be like for them, growing up believing their mother is a murderer when it's not tr—'

'No.' Becky stayed firm. 'At least they will see their father,' she said, returning to her seat. Perching on the edge, she turned away and stared out the window into the empty courtyard.

'But,—'

'Out,' shouted Will again. 'Or I'll report you to the police too when they arrive.'

Knowing there was no more she could do, Eleanor left. At least she had her answer. Becky's old boyfriend was the real criminal.

~

'Why doesn't he call?' Eleanor asked, frustration pouring out of her. She was picking her way through her crispy fried fish and chips.

'Who?' Darryl asked.

'Carl. I want to make sure he knows about Becky's boyfriend.'

'Why? Don't you think he knows his job?'

Eleanor turned on him abruptly.

'I'm just saying,' Darryl continued, 'have a bit of faith. They'll get the truth from her. Let's face it, he is a bit busy at the moment, what with three bodies, arson, and a hit and run in less than a week.'

'And everybody thinks it's my fault. I wish people would stop staring at me.'

Rain had brought people inside the pub, filling the normally quiet space. Darryl pulled his attention away from his meal and glanced around the room. He had to admit there was an air of disquiet.

'I guess word has got around and you've made quite a name for yourself.'

'Which one?' Eleanor sighed. 'I started off as a hussy, the married woman living with another man, then a grave robber. Now I'm the bounty hunter that everyone's going to hate for putting away the kindest woman in the county. I wish I could go back to those innocent hussy days.'

'I wanted to talk to you about that.'

This was the moment Darryl had been waiting for. He finished his last mouthful of fish and carefully placed his knife and fork on his plate, the palms of his hands sweating.

'Here he is,' Eleanor said suddenly and shifted in her seat impatiently.

DCI Carl Hanson searched the room, his gaze continuing past Eleanor and Darryl. Stopping at someone on the other side of the pub, he made his way across the room.

'He still doesn't want to talk to us yet, then,' Eleanor said sarcastically.

'Just let him do his job,' Darryl said. He paused, his nerves getting the better of him as he reached hesitantly for his jacket that hung over the back of his chair. 'I wanted to talk to you about something.'

A high-pitched squeal that sounded like a balloon having the air let out of it slowly came from the other side of the room. The pub went quiet as everyone stopped still. It took a moment for Darryl to realise the sound was a stifled scream. Everyone present watched DCI Hanson rise from his seat, drawn towards the only movement in the room. A woman next to him tried to join him but stumbled at the attempt. The DCI hastened to support her. The woman, now gently sobbing, was the owner of the tea-room, Jo. Carl held his arm comfortingly round her shoulders as they left the pub together. Silence had filled the room except for her quiet sobbing. Murmured conversations started again, filling the bar with an inquisitive energy. Darryl watched others in the bar, all with the same clandestine expressions, before turning back to Eleanor.

'Like I said, he's busy,' Darryl said, returning his jacket to the back of the chair. This wasn't the time for romantic gestures.

'I wonder what's happened,' Eleanor said. Her brow furrowed with concern.

'Who knows? I doubt it's anything to do with our place.'

'What if it is?' Eleanor said.

Darryl pushed his plate aside and gave Eleanor his full attention. 'OK, I'm ready for it.'

'Ready for what?'

'Your next wild theory. Though I've seen no evidence yet to support any of them.'

'I was right about the patio slabs.'

'You had so many theories about the patio slabs, you would have been very unlucky for one of them not to have been right.'

'I think,' Eleanor said defiantly, ignoring Darryl's remark, 'that one of the bodies they've found is Jo's dad. I know it's pure speculation,' she added from Darryl's look, 'but considering they believed he walked out soon after Miss Starling went missing, maybe he didn't. If he was getting close to the truth, and confronted Becky's boyfriend, he must have been willing to do anything to keep their secret, even if it was to kill again.'

'I'll admit, it works, but there's no evidence. You can't go making wild allegations and creating theories based on the most tenuous of circumstances.'

'A dead body is discovered in our house, then the officer in charge of the investigation comes to find Jo and she leaves distraught. I wouldn't call that tenuous.'

'He could have come to tell her that her cat had been run over.'

'In the middle of a murder investigation, he takes time out to inform an old friend that her cat is dead?'

'I'm just saying there could be other possibilities that you haven't considered.' Darryl paused, but the awkward silence that followed was uncomfortable, to say the least. 'So, saying you're right and one of the bodies is Jo's dad,' he continued, 'what would be your theory about the other one?'

'I don't know. Maybe we'll find out when he finally wants to speak to us.' Eleanor was losing her patience. 'Why hasn't he come to tell us about the bodies? After all, it's our house. I'm going to ring him.'

Darryl wanted to stop her, but had second thoughts. Her expression was determined. Thankfully, her attempt to contact the DCI came to nothing. She left a message asking for him to call her and she sat defeated. Laying her phone on the table in front of her, she sat nervously for another hour. Instead, Darryl's phone rang. It wasn't a number they recognised and so on answering Darryl assumed it would be the DCI. Instead, Richard introduced himself.

'Richard Atkins, the chief fire officer here,' came his thin, reedy voice down the phone.

'We've had results of our tests back and I'm sorry to say I can confirm your suspicions. This was a case of arson. Where are you now?'

Darryl told him they were both at the pub and confirmed with him they would not leave. Richard was currently at their house and wouldn't be leaving for a while yet. He had already spoken with DCI Hanson regarding their security and would be in touch.

By the time he got off the call, Eleanor was biting her lip with frustration.

'I'm calling him,' she said, snatching at her phone with determination. 'I can't bear the thought of Becky being in custody any longer than she has to be.'

Eleanor made the call and was put through to DCI Hanson straight away.

'I thought you may want to talk to us,' Eleanor said in her sweetest voice.

'You're absolutely right. I want to talk to you, but under the right circumstances. I do not expect you to be forcing your way in to questioning suspects, and gallivanting around the village as though nothing is wrong when I explicitly asked you to stay put—'

Darryl winced at the DCI's anger.

'There is no need to be upset with me,' Eleanor said smartly. 'I just wanted to let you know Becky didn't do it. Well, she did, but she didn't give the fatal second blow. That is something quite different to striking once as an accident. She's admitted to me she was there with her boyfriend, so he must have—'

'I'm sorry.'

Even Darryl could hear the gasp of exasperation at Eleanor's audacity, but Eleanor persevered.

'She didn't know about the other bodies, either,' Eleanor interrupted.

'Wh — what did you just say? How did you know about that?'

Eleanor hesitated. 'I can't say,' she replied.

'Mrs Garrett,' DCI Hanson said firmly down the phone. 'This isn't the first time you've had dealings with the police, is it? Last year, you were involved in another murder enquiry.'

'I wasn't exactly involved.' Eleanor's tone had changed. All pleasantries gone. 'Why are you checking up on me?'

'We look at everyone. It's a murder enquiry, and it seems to me that you need as much looking into as anyone else. You forced a confession from a dear friend of mine who I've known for most of my life. You take yourself and another civilian into a crime scene. You explicitly disobeyed my instruction of staying in the pub—'

'I thought it was more of a suggestion,' Eleanor added quietly.

'You have somehow managed to get information that you should not have,' the DCI continued.

'But it's our house. Surely we have a right to know what's going on in our own house.'

'And it's *my* investigation and I will let you know any information that I think you are entitled to in my own time. I've been doing some background research into both you and Mr Westwood, and it would seem you have earned quite a name for yourselves. Let me warn you, Mrs Garrett, everyone is under suspicion when it comes to a murder investigation. Just because you moved to the area three weeks ago doesn't mean you weren't here twenty years ago. Is Mr Westwood with you now?'

'Yes, he is.' Eleanor's tone was subdued.

'Then do me a favour and stay there. In fact, no, I want to see you before then. I'll let you travel from the pub to your house in an hour's time to meet me, but nowhere else. Prove to me you can stay out of trouble for that long. Do you understand me, Mrs Garrett?'

'Yes, I understand,' Eleanor whispered into her phone, and hung up. She opened her mouth to speak to Darryl.

'I heard,' Darryl said.

19

Nearly an hour later, Eleanor was still quiet. 'I'm only doing it for Becky,' she would say every now and again.

She had received quite a ticking off from the DCI and, though he wouldn't say it out loud, Darryl believed at least some of it was well deserved.

'I'm sorry,' she said finally to Darryl, not wanting to meet his eyes.

'Sorry for what?' he asked.

'You were right. I have gone a little overboard with this whole investigating thing. I don't know what I'm doing. I think I just needed something else to focus on instead of the house. The house,' she repeated angrily. 'It feels more like a prison.'

'I never realised that's how you felt about it.' Darryl reached for her hand across the table. 'We'll stay here. We'll stay here in the pub until it's done. Come on, it's been nearly an hour. Let's go and get Becky out of prison.'

They left the pub with renewed vigilance after Carl's warning and marched straight to the car.

'Becky has to give up the name of her boyfriend. She has to,' Eleanor cried.

Darryl pulled out of the pub car park and began the short distance home. He could see Eleanor in his peripheral vision frantically twisting her ring round her finger. The same concerned agitation ran through her as it did him.

'Will said they'd had a bad break-up. It's no wonder after an event like that. Whoever he was, he must have stayed around long enough to have killed Jo's dad and bury him in our house,' Eleanor said thoughtfully. 'Becky said he left the village soon after. Do you remember if Jo said how soon after Jenny went missing that her dad disappeared?'

'No, I don't think so,'

'The private investigator,' Eleanor suddenly exclaimed. 'I bet he's the other body they've found.'

'But that was years later,' Darryl said.

'I guess there's nothing to say he was killed locally,' Eleanor said, adjusting her sun visor. 'He could have caught up with the killer anywhere. And, if you've already successfully hidden two bodies, then surely that's the obvious place to hide another one. But then, none of this explains who has been after us *now*. At a push, I can imagine Becky breaking into the house with a pigeon, but arson? And we already know she can't drive, so it couldn't have been her that tried to run me down.'

'Do we know if she can't or won't drive? There is a difference.'

'Are you saying you think it was her?'

Darryl quickly changed his tack, fending off Eleanor's defensive tone. 'No, I was just thinking out loud. I guess the boyfriend could have come back to the village, or at least nearby. If nobody actually met him back then, they wouldn't know if the same guy turned up again a few years later.'

'That would work. This is getting complicated,' Eleanor sighed.

Darryl slowed as the road bent to the left, squinting at the blinding sun's reflection coming off the wet road, and intermittent flashes through the tree's branches from above. A turn right and another sharp left. This would be an unfortunate time for a tyre to burst, but that's what happened.

Darryl gripped the steering wheel and slammed on the brakes. The car skidded, ripping through the hazard tape that was stretched across the gaping hole in the bridge. Even though Darryl had slowed for the bend, the flimsy tape would not have helped them. The car plunged down the steep riverbank, over and over. Flashes of green through the windows as they tumbled. Screaming rang in his ears while glass shattered around him.

When the land rover finally came to rest on its roof, the windows had smashed, but the main framework was mainly intact. Darryl hung upside down, dazed. He shook his head, and his vision came back into focus. In the following two seconds he watched, helpless, as Eleanor slipped into unconsciousness.

'Eleanor, Eleanor.' His heart pounding, he struggled from his seat. Eventually releasing his seat belt, he fell, his arm above his head to lessen the impact. His head ducked under the water that had filled the upside-down roof space of the car. With the river running freely through the smashed windows, he scrambled his way upright.

'Eleanor!' he called again as he struggled towards her.

Reaching for her face, there was a slight motion at the touch of his hand. She was still alive. He tried to release her seat belt and prepared for her fall, but with her weight on the belt, it was impossible. He took her weight on his shoulders to enable him to push in the red button to free her. With one click, she landed on his shoulders, his knees buckling under the strain, and they fell sideways. That's when he felt the metal shard in his thigh. Adrenaline blocking the sensation of the small slither of metal until the pain burned through his right leg.

Eleanor's face ducked into the water, reviving her suddenly. She gasped for breath and fought to move, flailing her arms in panic.

'Eleanor,' Darryl forced his attention back to Eleanor, ignoring the pain in his thigh. 'Eleanor, it's OK.'

'What happened? Where are we?'

'The car had a blowout. I lost control. We need to get out,' he said as calmly as he could.

Thankfully, the warm spring had kept the river low and the rain from today hadn't been enough to fill the ten-metre-wide riverbed, but still it was deepening inside the car. It had already inched its way up to just below Darryl's knees. Eleanor grabbed at something in the water by her feet. It was her handbag. She reached inside for her phone, but it was sodden. She eagerly pressed every button, but the screen remained blank. Darryl's own phone was in his jacket pocket and, confined by the lack of space, he struggled to reach in and grab it. Finally, he pulled it from his pocket, only to see an enormous crack across the screen. Not always the end of a phone's life, but for Darryl's, it was.

Suddenly the car shifted around them, and they lurched with the movement, holding on to whatever they could around them. It took a moment to realise what was happening. The car was sliding on its roof. Moving downstream from the build-up of water against one side, pushing the car along the riverbed. They could only try to keep themselves stable; escaping the car while it was moving would have been impossible. Darryl, trying to keep his weight on his left leg and ignore the pain searing through his thigh, couldn't take his eyes off Eleanor. The pain of a cut in his leg he could cope with. Losing Eleanor, he couldn't. She had already lost consciousness once, there was no guarantee it wouldn't happen again. He watched her intently. Watched as she struggled to keep herself upright with the sway of the car. Her legs periodically collapsing at the knees. The car finally came to a stop. Jolting suddenly as though hitting against rocks in the river. Tentatively, they moved. Trying not to destabilise the car from its resting place, they searched for an exit. Trying the doors seemed futile. Eleanor's was visibly crushed and jammed. Darryl tried his own. He could push it open an inch with his shoulder behind it, but then it stopped. With the strength in his left leg and adrenaline pumping through him, he was able to kick it open. Well aware that the sudden force could have started the car sliding again, but it was a risk they had to take.

'Are you hurt?' asked Eleanor, observing the blood on his jeans. Panic in her voice.

'Just a scratch,' he quipped. 'Nothing more than we've had to deal with before.'

Eleanor hesitated. He could see in her eyes that she didn't believe him. After a moment, she turned from him, scooped some water in her hands, and threw it over her face. At any other time, Darryl would have insisted she took it easy after such a horrific accident, but there was no way Darryl could do this without her. She needed to be awake; she needed to focus. And she knew it. Darryl took the opportunity, while she was distracted, to climb out of the car, knowing he wouldn't be able to do it without grimacing from pain. It was outside the car that movement from the bushes caught his attention.

'Hey,' he shouted. 'Is somebody there? We need help.'

Eleanor joined him, holding on to the side of the car. Together they searched, but the sun was low and the bushes that grew half-way up the steep bank were in darkness.

There was no reply, only silence until Eleanor's scream. A short, high-pitched cry that came almost simultaneously with a flash of light. A shot from the bushes and what seemed like an explosion across the underside of the car. They both dived back towards the main body of the car, ducking down for protection.

'It's him. The boyfriend accomplice.' Eleanor grabbed Darryl's hand and squeezed. 'What if—'

Another shot came, and they moved further round the car, keeping close and low.

'Nobody met or even saw this new boyfriend,' Eleanor gabbled, 'only for him to disappear soon after. What if he didn't disappear?'

'I don't understand,' said Darryl.

'And then, there's Fred Fletcher,' Eleanor's eyes widened.

Eleanor's random thoughts and mindless rambling were worrying. The effects of concussion on Darryl's mind.

'The man who was killed here,' she went on. '*He* had a blowout on this bridge, which sent him over the edge.'

Darryl suddenly saw the relevance. 'That's too much of a coincidence.'

He had seen nothing on the road that would cause a blowout, but then it was difficult to see anything, blinded as he had been by the sun. He peered round the car, trying to see his front tyre for any telltale signs. His heart pounding at the thought of a gun's barrel pointing directly at him. He managed a glimpse before another shot came. He ducked, closing his eyes with hope as his only shield against any stray pellets. They scattered across the underside of the car, indenting themselves into the metal. He turned back to Eleanor. His muscles were so tight he struggled to breathe, let alone speak.

'So, who was this boyfriend?' he growled.

The tyre was shredded, and he had just managed to see a nail sticking out of the rubber. One nail wouldn't have caused that much damage, but a handful of nails? Or maybe even enough to cover the road. For all Eleanor's crazy theories, he had to admit; she was right. The accomplice was still here.

'It has to be Shaun,' Eleanor said

Darryl couldn't help himself and let out a small burst of laughter. 'Now, I know you don't like him, I don't either, but you can't go accusing him of murder because he's a sleazy letch.'

'It's not just because I don't like him. Think about it. I bet he started a fling with Becky, telling her it was true love, but not to say anything until he had left Alison. That's why nobody met or saw this mysterious boyfriend. They already knew him. And, in true Casanova style, a couple of weeks later, he goes back to Alison as if nothing has happened. Leaving Becky broken hearted. Jenny's murder was probably a good excuse to break it off.'

Darryl could see her logic, but still unconvinced. There were too many other questions that needed answering. Why would Becky make up a story about her boyfriend leaving? And why kill Fred what's-his-name? But now wasn't the time for those questions, as another shot came at them. The sound came from slightly further downstream. The shooter had moved position to get a better view. Darryl and Eleanor moved further round the car, stopping where they hoped they were safe, and clung to each other.

'I'm sorry to say, I think you need a bit more than that. I'm not saying I don't believe you, but you need some kind of evidence.'

'The other day, in the pub,' Eleanor interrupted, 'Stella knocked over her coffee and Shaun was very quick to help clear up the mess. But what struck me was Stella's reaction. There was no doubt that she doesn't like him. He said it went back to their school days, but what if it was for something more recent?'

'Like a murdering spree.'

Another shot rang out. The shooter having moved again. He had double-backed and was around the other side of the car, moving silently closer to them. Determined to make sure they didn't leave this place alive.

'The list,' Eleanor suddenly exclaimed as they scrambled their way round the car again. 'I had the list of suspects on the table when they cleared up after the coffee. I had assumed the landlord had taken it away with everything else after clearing up, but Shaun must have taken it and thought we were on to him. That would certainly give him a motive for trying to run me down. Have I convinced you yet?'

Darryl hesitated, remembering his encounter with Alison in the shop. Maybe she wasn't asking questions because she was guilty. Her furtive glances towards the doorway could easily have been her hoping that Shaun didn't enter to find she had her own suspicions.

'For God's sake, Darryl. We don't have time for evidence. It was twenty years ago and we don't have the luxury of a laboratory. We are stuck in the middle of a river being shot at.'

Darryl had to admit, her theory sounded more plausible by the second. He nodded and accepted that she was right. Carl was trying his best to find the culprit, but it wasn't Carl at risk of becoming the next victim. The rain started again like an insult. As if they weren't soaked and cold enough. His leg throbbed; there was no doubt it would need medical attention, and soon. He watched Eleanor as she tried to peer round the car in the shooter's direction. A sinking feeling of resignation inside him. There was no way out.

∼

Eleanor tentatively peered through any gap she could find, trying to work out where Shaun was hiding in the bushes. She turned back just in time to see Darryl's right hand reach towards the upper left-hand side of his jacket, where the jewellery box still laid hidden. He laughed, a slightly maniacal laugh.

'I had this crazy idea,' he said. 'Eleanor, I have something for you.'

'I don't think now is a good time.' How could he even think of proposing at a time like this? More to the point, how could she turn him down at a time like this?

'Considering the situation,' he said, 'I think it's an excellent time.'

'Considering the situation,' Eleanor repeated, 'I think our time would be better spent working out how we're going to get out of this.'

He had been reaching into his jacket, but she was glad to see that his hand was empty when he pulled it out again. Pushing her relief to one side, she turned her attention back to examining their surroundings. Would they be able to make it to the opposite bank? The river was rising higher as the rain fell harder. Shivering from the cold, she saw no other choice.

~

Eleanor was right. Darryl shook himself from his self-pity and focused on their escape. The bank on the other side of the river led up a gentle slope to a woodland only a couple of metres away from the water's edge. There she would have more chance of escape. There, she could be safe.

'Do you think you can make it to those trees?' Darryl asked.

'Can you?' Eleanor glanced towards Darryl's thigh, where blood covered his trousers.

'It's our only hope.' Darryl shivered involuntarily. The rain dripping from his hair and down his neck. 'If we keep low, we might be able to stay sheltered by the car for most of it. If we can see where he is...'

Darryl crept round the car and towards the shooter's line of sight. A shot fired, hitting the water slightly to his right, and a flash appeared in the bushes closer to the water's edge. Closer to them. Only two or so metres up the steep bank opposite where the bushes grew thicker in density. If his intention was to reach them, the bushes would slow his descent.

'Good,' Darryl said. 'The closer he is, the more shelter we can get from the car. You go first. Remember, keep low for your best chance of staying out of sight.'

'We should go together.'

Darryl hesitated. Only a slight hesitation, but it was there.

'I'll be right behind you,' he said.

'Darryl?' she said questioningly.

'I'll be right behind you, but move fast. We need to make as narrow a line of sight as possible.' He wouldn't be able to keep up with this wound in his leg, but he had to help Eleanor make it to the trees. The best he could hope for was to be a distraction.

Eleanor agreed and crouched down into the water and crept forward. The water gently changed its course to run round her. The rain minimising any telltale ripples of her movement.

Darryl kept an eye on the line of sight between her and the clump of bushes. She had almost made it to the bank when Darryl made a slight movement to the right and immediately pulled back again, drawing the shooter's focus away from Eleanor. The shot missed Darryl's arm and small splashes appeared in the water only a metre away.

'Run,' Darryl called, and watched as she slipped and scrambled up the mud on the riverbank and into the trees. Another shot rang out a moment later, to Eleanor's side. The shooter losing accuracy in favour of speed. Darryl could only imagine her relief as she made the safety of the trees, and then her rage when she realised he wasn't with her.

20

Eleanor stumbled into the protection of the trees, slipping in the wet mud. The few seconds of silence as she scrambled for the riverbank came as a revelation. The gun was a shotgun. Two cartridges used before it needed to be reloaded. Just those few precious moments were enough for her to scramble behind a large tree. Falling against the hard, thick trunk, she gasped for breath. Almost instantly, she noticed the other silence. The silence that told her she was alone.

Being careful to stay out of sight, she peered round the tree, terrified of what she would see. She could already picture in her mind Darryl's body floating away in the river. The sight of him, still by the car, clutching at his thigh brought tears to her eyes, part from relief and part from despair. Blood covered his hands and trousers. *She* had only just managed to make it to the trees. How could Darryl with that wound in his leg? Looking around her for inspiration, Eleanor saw some small rocks across the river further downstream that could easily be used as stepping-stones. And that gave her an idea.

With no time for self-pity, Eleanor backed into the darkness and shelter of the trees. The killer had clearly hoped the crash would kill them, and they would become just two more victims of Black Spot Bridge. Nonetheless, he had come prepared. Even if they had gunshot wounds, he would find a way to hide his guilt. After all, he had got away with at least four murders already. What difference would a couple more make? But Eleanor was banking on the fact that he needed both of them dead. Darryl had been a distraction for her, so she would do the same for him.

She crept silently through the woods, staying back in the darkness of their cover. She purposefully snapped a twig or two along the way. Not too many, or he would know what she was doing. He had to think how clever he was being; tracking her down towards the few steppingstones that were still accessible across the river. There needed to be a reason she would have been sneaking downstream instead of up and towards the road. The steppingstones gave this reason. An attempt to cross the river quickly in the hope of stopping him. His shotgun focused on her rather than Darryl.

Coming closer to the bank, she found the perfect spot for what she needed. Hidden from the shooter's view on the other side of the river, but within Darryl's. He was still clutching at his thigh, his face distorted in pain. When she emerged into position, she saw him shaking his head. He had clearly been tracking her too and understood what she was going to do. He may not like it, but she wasn't keen on the alternative either.

∼

The river was rising higher as the rain fell harder, building up around the land rover. Darryl leaned against the car for support, with the cold water now running around his knees. Why didn't she just leave? She could get help. Get help? That wouldn't happen. Not in time to help him anyway, but at least she could get away and be safe. Unfortunately, the determination on her face told him she would not give up that easily.

The land rover slid behind him, and he lost his balance. Stumbling in the water as the car moved again, both from the build-up of the water and Darryl's weight against it. The car was unstable on the loose gravel of the riverbed. A sudden rush of hope. No matter what Eleanor did to distract the shooter, Darryl could never make it across to the bank in time. The distance was too far for him to manage with his injured leg. But what if he could shorten that distance? Using the car's momentum, he pulled it as far as he could, twisting it in the water further downstream and closer to the bank. Keeping as low as he could and out of sight. With effort and determination, he moved the large land rover another two or three metres closer to the bank before it jammed against some larger rocks. If Eleanor was going to do this, then he had to give himself the best possible chance. It was only another metre or so before the edge of the river and here the water was shallow enough to make running easier. He had seen how Eleanor had struggled in the mud, though, and was under no illusion that this was going to be easy. He readied himself and turned back to Eleanor, judging the distance between her and the shooter to be at least forty, maybe even fifty metres. Not knowing the range of a shotgun, he hoped that would be enough. He nodded to show he was ready. It was now or never.

~

Eleanor watched in confusion, but it didn't take long to see the benefits of Darryl's pushing and pulling. The car rocked on its roof from Darryl's efforts to move it across the river and closer to the bank. From her position, she could see some larger rocks sticking out through the water just a short distance away, and she willed the car to miss them. But she knew it would be too much to ask. It jolted to a halt and, after Darryl gave it an extra push, it was clear it wasn't going to move any further. He stood facing her; his hair flat against his head in the rain; pale with exhaustion. He gave her the OK with a nod and she took a deep breath, preparing herself.

Two shots and then reload. This had become her mantra, and she tried to focus her thoughts on this and not on all the possibilities that could go wrong. The slippery mud that could slow them down. Would the distance between her and Darryl be enough to slow the killer's shot and affect his aim? But there was no other choice; she would not leave him.

Two shots and then reload. She ran. From one tree to another, across a clearing where Shaun would easily see her had he been tracking her down the river as she had planned. The sound of a shot burst in her ears, but it was badly aimed. She hoped he would keep his focus on her, believing she was heading for the steppingstones, but there was a movement in the bushes. Another shot fired and Darryl yelled out in pain. She double backed, terrified that her plan had failed. Darryl was already out of sight; he must have at least made it into the trees. She ran through the woods and further back into the cover of darkness, making the most of the few seconds it took to reload the shotgun. It was only moments until shot embed themselves into the trunks of nearby trees as she ran past. Splinters of wood flying into the air.

The sun was below the horizon now, and her eyes were adjusting to the dim light. Up ahead she could make out the shape of Darryl sitting against a tree, his back to the river. The shooting stopped, but there was a movement in the foliage. The shooter was forcing his way through the dense bushes, almost at the river, as she reached Darryl.

'Are you alright?' she asked.

'He clipped my ankle,' Darryl said through gritted teeth.

Eleanor jumped at the sound of a splash and they both went quiet, staring at each other. There was no doubt what that sound meant. The continuous splashing of wading through water continued, coming closer.

'Go,' Darryl implored. 'Leave me. I can't walk, let alone run.'

'I'm not leaving you,' she said, 'and it's not up for debate. Can you stand? I'll help you.' Crouching by his side, she tried to lift him to his feet.

'Eleanor, you have to go.' He stared deep into her eyes. 'You are the only chance of stopping him. He's been killing for years and if you don't stop him, he will carry on for many more years. It's more important that you stop him than to try and save me and we both get killed.'

Eleanor shook her head. There was no way she could do it. Everything he said made sense, but could she really leave him to die?

~

The wading footsteps became tiny splashes, and then the squelch of mud. The killer had reached the river's edge.

'Go, please, go.' Darryl's eyes, full of tears, could no longer see. Eleanor's face was a blur.

The thought of her dying was too much to bear. He was the one who originally wanted to investigate. Had he manipulated her into joining him? Seeing her back away silently filled him with relief. As she turned and disappeared into the darkness, moving towards the road, DCI Carl Hanson appeared, a shotgun jammed under his arm.

'You just wouldn't leave, would you?' Carl said, tears streaming down his face. 'All you had to do was to move away or leave it for us to deal with. That's what the police do, after all.'

Darryl struggled to make sense of what he was seeing. Carl was the accomplice? 'You mean police like you? You've been covering it up all these years. Killing more and more people—'

'I don't want to kill you,' Carl roared. 'I didn't want to kill anyone, but she keeps on—' He struggled to look Darryl in the eye. Shaking his head, he whispered, 'I have to protect Becky. She—' He choked through his tears. Taking a deep breath, he composed himself and his tone turned angry. 'Some people just don't know when it's better to leave things alone. You should have just left. But no, you insisted on doing your own little investigation.'

Darryl didn't see the face of the man he was expecting, but he also didn't see the face of a ruthless murderer, hardened to the inevitable act of killing. Instead, he saw a desperate man. Tear-stained and ragged.

'You're doing all of this for Becky? Becky is telling you to do this?' Darryl's voice trembled with fear. 'She's in prison now. You don't have to do anything for her.' Darryl's plea was met with a laugh. 'If you want to help her, the only thing you can do now is hand yourself in. You don't have to do this,' he implored. But there was no reasoning with him.

'You don't understand.' The shotgun wavered with Carl's shuddering sobs. He lifted the barrel and pointed it directly at Darryl's head. The tip of the gun only a few inches away.

Two large, black, endless holes were all Darryl could focus on. Not wanting to see what was coming, he squeezed his eyes tight. All pain had dissipated. His only thought now was of fear. He didn't want to die. He tried to focus his thoughts on Eleanor. She would escape. She would stop the killings and there would be a purpose behind his death. Nevertheless, he would never see her again. Images of his daughters forced their way into his head. The thought of never seeing them again tore at his heart and his chest ached unbearably.

Waiting for the darkness, his senses heightened with fear, he jumped at the sound of a thud. And then, on the ground by his side, another larger thud. He tentatively opened his eyes and saw Eleanor with a large rock in her hands and Carl unconscious on the ground.

'I told you it wasn't up for debate,' she said.

Darryl released a full flood of tears with a laugh of relief. The DCI was still breathing, but he was going to have one hell of a headache when he woke up.

～

Eleanor woke with a start. Her mind reliving the final few minutes before help came. She had backed away from Darryl through the trees, leaving him to his fate with Shaun. Except it wasn't Shaun. It was DCI Carl Hanson that emerged from the river and into the darkness of the trees. At that moment, a million questions were answered. Carl had struck that second fatal blow. Whoever broke in to their house didn't have to outrun him, he only needed to make it look like they did. Joining the police force meant he was well-placed for covering up anything that may arise. Marrying Stella was probably no more than pure manipulation on his part. She was so devoted to him, she would do anything, such as spread a few rumours of ghosts to help keep people from buying the place, hold back on her enthusiasm to sell, or let him know if anybody was interested. He knew she and Darryl were searching for the killer, as she herself kept insisting on telling him. He knew they would be travelling down this road, over Black Spot bridge at this particular time. It all made sense.

But whether Shaun or Carl, at that point in time, didn't matter. She couldn't do it. Leaving Darryl to die wasn't an option. She searched frantically for something she could use as a weapon and found a large rock. Though her arms were weak from exhaustion, determination and adrenaline helped her to lift it above her head and bring it down on Carl. She watched him fall to the ground in front of her.

She had gone from terror to relief in a moment, but still there was no time to stop. Carl was alive and could wake at any moment. She had to get Darryl away.

Together, they struggled up the hill. Eleanor supporting Darryl as best she could. They were almost at the road when they heard a car pulling up. Its headlights lighting the road ahead of them. Richard Atkins, the Chief Fire Officer, emerged from the car and peered over the edge of the road with a torch, down into the river. The torn tape blowing wildly in the wind. Eleanor called to him, but her voice was hardly more than a whisper. The muscles in her body almost collapsing under Darryl's weight. She called again, though this time it was more of a scream out of desperation that he would hear. He ran to them and took over supporting Darryl's weight, helping him back towards the car. Eleanor's knees finally gave way, and she collapsed to the ground. That was the last she could remember.

She had now woken to the sound of murmuring voices. She opened her eyes and saw a woman in police uniform talking with a doctor.

The desperation she had felt, backing away from Darryl, leaving him to certain death; the rage that consumed her as she lifted the rock above her head. These emotions were still raw after her dream, as though she had lived that moment again and again. And now, a policewoman stood guard at the far end of her hospital bed, in discussions with the doctor.

Just how hard had she hit DCI Hanson with that rock? Had she gone through all that only to be arrested herself for murder?

21

Eleanor laid rigid in her bed. Hardly daring to breathe. A subconscious move caught the attention of both the policewoman and the doctor.

'Mrs Garrett,' the policewoman said. Her face was stern.

Eleanor immediately gabbled, fear taking hold of her tongue. 'He- he was trying to kill us. I had to do it. He was about to shoot Darryl. Where- where is Darryl? Is he alright? I had to do it. He killed everyone—'

'Mrs Garrett, please,' the policewoman said calmly, holding a hand in the air in a quiet gesture. 'I'm Superintendent Calver. I've heard that you've had some trouble with one of my Detective Chief Inspectors.'

'I don't think trouble is quite the word I'd use,' Eleanor mumbled in reply.

'No, you're quite right.' The sternness returned to Superintendent Calver's face. 'But you have nothing to worry about now. He's in police custody, *honest* police, and I have already spoken with Mr Westwood while you were sleeping—'

'He's alright?'

'He's on the mend.' The superintendent frowned slightly at

the interruption. 'And I wanted to come and apologise in person for what both you and Mr Westwood have been through.'

'Oh,' was all Eleanor could say, relief consuming her.

'He was always an exemplary officer. Determined to prove himself, though it would seem he was actually just determined to stay in the perfect position to protect his secret. He fooled us all.'

Eleanor wasn't listening. Her focus was elsewhere.

'Can I see Darryl?' she asked tentatively. She had no use of an apology from the police. She only wanted to see Darryl, to hold his hand, to hear his voice, knowing they were safe again.

'You'll have to ask the doctor that one.'

They both turned to the doctor questioningly.

'If you feel up to it, then I see no problem,' the doctor replied.

Eleanor didn't have far to go to reach Darryl's room. The doctor's instructions were easy to follow. On the way down the corridor, she saw Stella. Her back towards Eleanor, but there was no mistaking it was her with her bouncing blonde curls and small stature. She was talking with a police officer standing guard outside a door.

'What harm can it do?' Stella was saying to the policeman as he flicked through the pages of a book and then shook it upside down. 'I have just spent three hours stuck in a grubby little room being interrogated. Being told the most awful things and now I want to see my husband. I won't believe he did this till I hear it from him.'

Eleanor saw the policeman look behind her. Stella had noticed it too. Following their eyeline, Eleanor saw Superintendent Calver had also left her room and was in the corridor.

'I have to hear it from him,' Stella pleaded. 'I only want five minutes.'

Superintendent Calver nodded. Her permission granted.

'I'll even leave my bag with you and just take the book and photograph. You know he can't bear to be away from me for too long, and this photograph will bring him just a little joy in his time of need.'

Stella was used to getting her own way, and Eleanor could hear the strain in her voice. She couldn't help but feel sorry for Stella as she passed behind her in the corridor. The photograph she had clutched in her hands wasn't any old photograph, but one from their wedding day in a sleek, glass-fronted frame. The poor woman still didn't realise she was more besotted with her husband than he was with her; that her entire marriage had been a pretense.

Darryl's room was further along the same corridor. She opened the door, and his broad grin lifted her heart. He was sitting in bed finishing a coffee. An empty biscuit wrapper was on the table that had been pulled across the bed.

'Do you think we will ever get through an entire year without at least one of us ending up in the hospital?' Eleanor said, pushing the table to one side and sitting on the edge of his bed; taking a tight hold of his hand.

'Or some maniac trying to kill us?' Darryl replied.

'Thank God it's all over,' Eleanor sighed with relief. Her shoulders ached from the release of her tension.

'Yeah,' Darryl agreed, but there was something in his tone that sounded like doubt.

'You don't think it is over?' Eleanor asked tentatively.

'I've been thinking about something Carl said.'

'Oh, really? I don't think I'm interested in anything DCI Hanson had to say,' Eleanor exclaimed.

'He was really torn up about killing us.'

'My heart bleeds for him,' she said, astonished at the sentence that just came out of Darryl's mouth.

'No, listen. He said he *had* to do it. Then he said that "she keeps—" before he pulled himself back from saying anymore.'

'So, you think Becky made him kill the others to protect her?' Eleanor said incredulously. 'No, I can't believe she would make him kill more people when she was already suffering so much over the death of Jenny. And I'm certain she didn't even know about the other deaths. He was doing it to protect himself. He was the one who hit her the second time. *He* killed Jenny.'

'No, I don't think Becky made him, but something's not right. When I asked him about Becky, he just laughed.'

A switch flicked in Eleanor's head. She had been a fool.

'You're right. Why try to kill us now?' she said, trying to keep up with her thoughts. 'Killing us wouldn't protect Becky anymore. She had already been caught, and she wasn't going to give up his name. Unless...' Eleanor's words drifted off. There were too many scenarios playing in her head to think straight until the image of the photograph came into her head. Stella's precious wedding photograph in a sleek, modern frame. Stella had told the guard she only wanted five minutes with her husband. Five minutes for what? He was about to go to prison, probably for life. Surely, you'd want more than five minutes.

'Unless what?' asked Darryl impatiently.

'Stella,' Eleanor exclaimed.

'Stella? What about her?'

'The *she* is Stella.' Eleanor left Darryl with a puzzled expression on his face. 'I'll explain later.'

She turned back into the corridor and could see the uniformed police officer still diligently standing guard outside DCI Hanson's room. The door opened and Stella walked out. Eleanor's footsteps quickened.

'He's just going to have a little sleep,' she could hear Stella telling the officer, standing guard. 'So, if you could make sure he's not disturbed, I'd be very grateful.'

'What have you done?' Eleanor called along the hall. She ran the last few steps and attempted to barge her way through the door. Both the police officer and Stella held her back.

'I'm afraid my husband needs rest,' Stella said. '*Somebody* hit him over the head with a large rock.'

'He was trying to kill us,' Eleanor said incredulously.

'He has now fully explained the situation to me and I have forgiven him. So, if you could please leave us both in peace, our lives would be much the better for it.' She gave a piercing stare at Eleanor before turning away and walking towards the exit. Her head held high.

'You've forgiven him?' Eleanor called down the corridor.

Superintendent Calver had seen the commotion and was making her way towards them. Eleanor had to think quickly. She couldn't let Stella leave, and the police officer wasn't going to let her into Carl's room, either.

'Why did you want our house, Stella?'

Stella ignored her and kept on walking. As she walked further away, Eleanor's voice became louder, wanting to attract the attention of others around her. Only making a scene would stop Stella now.

'You like everything that's modern. Why would you want Rushmere Cottage? Is it because you knew the bodies were hidden there?'

Stella's shoulders stiffened as she continued to walk towards the lift at the end of the corridor. Eleanor's loud insinuations were working. Staff and visitors dotted the wide hospital corridor and all of them were now paying attention to her. Superintendent Calver stepped out in front of Stella, stopping her from going any further. Looking down on her with an inquisitive gaze.

'I guess it would have been the best way for you to make sure they were never found,' Eleanor went on. 'Neither Carl nor

Becky hit Miss Starling that second time, did they? It was you. You've been blackmailing him for the last twenty years, making him and Becky believe they had killed her, but it was you. I've noticed you have a very manipulative way about you. You knew Darryl was in the tearoom with another woman. You purposely led me that way, putting ideas of infidelity in my head.'

Eleanor paused. The crowd in the corridor was growing bigger and Stella seemed to get smaller under the staring eyes of Superintendent Calver.

'Did they know you were there that day?' Eleanor continued. 'Or were you watching your beloved Carl like some stalker? I guess they must have gone inside the house at some point to get the suitcase of clothes. Did she regain consciousness while they were gone? Is that when you did it?'

'Mrs Garrett,' the Superintendent called, nudging Stella gently back along the corridor, 'I think maybe we should have a quiet conversation. Back in your room, perhaps?'

Eleanor, who was still being held by the police officer outside Carl's room, panicked. 'No, you need to check on DCI Hanson.'

'He won't be going anywhere, but I must insist on you accompanying me.' The Superintendent was firm while keeping a close eye on Stella as they came closer.

Eleanor turned her attention back to Stella and continued; she needed to get some kind of reaction. Something that would make them believe that Carl was in danger.

'You persuaded him to kill Jo's father, didn't you? As the officer in charge of Miss Starling's disappearance, was he getting too close to the truth? If Miss Starling's body had been found back then, they would have discovered the truth of what you had done. And after you had manipulated Carl to be with you, you couldn't bear for him to find out, and so soon.' Again, Eleanor paused. Stella remained quiet, but Eleanor could see her aloofness was strained. They were getting closer along the corridor and so she continued quickly. 'Years later, when a private investigator came snooping, was it easier to convince Carl to do it a second time? He had already killed once for you.' Still, Stella said nothing. Eleanor needed something to make her crack.

'Do you really think Carl killed them for you? Surely you must know it was all to protect Becky.'

Stella's reserve finally cracked. Screaming at the mention of Becky's name, she lurched towards Eleanor, but Superintendent Calver's quick movements pulled her back.

'And you're still making him kill for you,' Eleanor went on, as they came further down the corridor. 'Fred Fletcher, it's funny he had a blowout at exactly the same place we did on Black Spot Bridge. A few nails and pieces of sharp metal thrown across the road at just the right time. The road is used so little it would have been easy to judge. Did he want to buy Rushmere Cottage? Why else would he have been on that road? But you couldn't let that happen, could you? You had to stop him.'

'Mrs Garrett,' the Superintendent interrupted, but Eleanor went on.

'You broke into our house and let loose the pigeon. We thought it was just convenient when Carl turned up, but it wasn't a coincidence at all, was it? You didn't need to be fast to get away, as he wasn't even going to try to catch you. It was all one big show.' The Superintendent and Stella had reached her now, but the anger in Superintendent Calver's eyes didn't stop her.

Eleanor turned to the guard, still holding on to her arms.

'Please,' she begged. 'Check on DCI Hanson. She's been manipulating him for all these years.'

After a slight pause and a nod from the superintendent, the officer opened the door. Blood was seeping across the bedsheet.

'Shit,' the police officer exclaimed and immediately let go of Eleanor, pushing her out of his way, scrambling to get into the room. Uniformed doctors and nurses swarmed from all directions and followed him in. Eleanor stood back to let them through, but before she did, she had enough time to see her suspicion had been correct. The framed wedding photograph was lying on the bedside cabinet, the glass front smashed. A broken shard of glass was lying by his right hand while his left wrist oozed with blood. If they had left him any longer, Stella would probably have succeeded in her attempt at making it look like suicide.

While the commotion continued in the small room, DCI Hanson opened his eyes and stared coldly at Eleanor.

'I'm sorry,' he said, so quietly Eleanor struggled to hear it. 'I didn't want to hurt you. I didn't want to hurt anyone. Please, just leave me.'

'You still love Becky, don't you?' Eleanor asked him.

He lowered his eyes, but it was all that was needed.

'That bloody woman.' Stella burst into a rage. 'Why wouldn't you just love me? Becky this, Becky that. What about me? No one could love you more than I do. I was even going to help you with her escape and yet still you—' Stella finished the sentence with a scream.

Eleanor noticed the superintendent's focus moved quickly to DCI Hanson. Aiding a prisoner to escape. Another offence to add to his list of crimes.

'What do I have to do to make you love me? Do you think she would have stayed with you after she'd found out you can't have children?' Stella continued, spitting out her words. 'She's selfish. She would have turned you out.'

'But—' Eleanor began before thinking twice about speaking, and she bit her lip.

'But what?' Stella snapped.

Eleanor and Carl looked at each other. After a brief pause, he gave her a nod.

Eleanor was still unsure whether to say what she suspected. After all, it would affect more than just those present.

'After refusing to give her accomplice's name,' Eleanor began tentatively, 'Becky said that at least the children will see their father. Of course they will because they'll be living with their father.' She turned back to Carl. 'But they won't, will they? Will told us that his children were a miracle, as the doctors had said he wouldn't be able to have children. That's what Becky meant, isn't it? You are their father. She would never give up your name as the accomplice, because at least they will see you, even if they can't see their mother. And, of course, because she still loves you.'

He turned his head away.

'Carl?' Stella called. 'You said you couldn't have children. I don't understand.'

Though she couldn't see his face, Eleanor could tell he was crying. His shoulders shuddered with his tears.

'I didn't *want* children,' he sobbed. He turned back and stared at Stella. 'with you,' he finished defiantly.

Stella immediately burst into a noisy sob. 'He did it. He killed them all.'

'No,' Eleanor shouted over her ruckus. 'You killed Miss Starling.'

Stella stopped abruptly. There were no tears streaking down her face. Her outburst had all been for show. The entire corridor had gone silent.

'Jennifer Nightingale was her real name,' Eleanor went on, finally proud that she had found justice for both Jennifer and her sister Amelia. 'She'd lived most of her life in fear. When she had finally found some happiness, you took advantage of an accident and killed her. Then you blackmailed Carl into spending the rest of his life with you.'

Stella stared at her defiantly.

'He may have married you,' Eleanor continued, 'but he never loved you.'

Stella opened her mouth to retaliate, but Superintendent Calver intervened. 'It's been a long time since I've had the pleasure of personally arresting someone. And, believe me, this is a pleasure.'

'They're not needed,' Stella snapped, struggling wildly as the Superintendent clicked handcuffs around her wrists.

'Maybe not for you,' Superintendent Calver whispered in her ear, 'but they are for me. In all my years in the force, I don't think an arrest has ever given me so much satisfaction.'

∼

Eleanor returned to Darryl's room. If it hadn't been so tragic, she would have walked with a spring in her step. She couldn't wait to tell him what had happened; that she had worked it out.

She spent the following half an hour pacing the length of Darryl's bed, regaling the event. How Carl had done everything out of love for Becky, though Stella had convinced herself he had done it for her. How they had planned to help Becky escape, and Carl's compliance as he laid there bleeding. Welcoming death now he had lost Becky forever.

'I still don't understand why they made up the story of Becky's non-existent boyfriend,' Darryl said.

'I'm guessing,' Eleanor admitted, 'but I don't think Carl could bring himself to admit to Becky that Stella knew what they had done and that he would be blackmailed for the rest of his life. I think he probably told her it was for the best if they split. If they weren't together, they couldn't be suspects together.

No one would have suspected Becky on her own, but she and Carl together would have been different. And this way, if Carl was caught, he could easily keep Becky's name out of it.'

'But that still doesn't explain the bad break-up story. They could have just separated.'

'It would have devastated Becky. She needed to be able to grieve. Both for the death of her friend and for losing Carl. The story gave her something to latch her grief on to.'

Eleanor slumped onto Darryl's bed, exhaustion coming over her suddenly. 'Please, no more investigating,' she implored.

'Only Romans,' he said with a broad grin. There was a moment's pause before Darryl spoke again. 'Eleanor, I want to ask you something.'

Immediately, the familiar knot appeared in her stomach and her high spirits plummeted. It wasn't that she didn't love Darryl, but to take such an enormous step as to marrying him felt like a betrayal of Nick's memory. She couldn't shut Nick out of her life entirely.

'Could you pass me my jacket?' he asked.

'I can't stay for long. The doctor wanted to see me again,' she said as she reached slowly for his jacket, where it had been hung on a rail by the radiator to dry after last night's ordeal.

'It won't take a moment. Just something for you to think about.' Darryl took the jacket and searched for the front opening.

'You'll need to ask me later.' Eleanor edged towards the door. The excitement in his voice scared her. 'I'd better get back now. I've been too long as it is.'

She left the room quickly, his voice calling after her. Darryl was right. She needed to think about it. She needed to think about how she could turn him down without upsetting him, or even losing him completely. How could she explain to him that this wasn't something she was ready to even think about yet?

22

'Eleanor, sit,' Darryl said, as though commanding a dog.

She had been fidgety ever since they had returned from the hospital. Constantly jumping up if he needed anything. Accommodating his every want, as though it was her fault that he was in this condition. Even if he wanted nothing, she would find something. She was about to jump up and head off again, but he took hold of her hands and pulled her back, forcing her to sit next to him on the side of their bed. He had already taken the jewellery box from his jacket and had it ready, tucked in his jeans pocket. She would not get away this time.

'No,' he said firmly. 'Whatever it is, it can wait. I've been out of hospital for two weeks, and I've hardly seen you. Considering we're living in one room at the moment, that's really quite an achievement.'

'You're the one that keeps going out, down to the house and leaving me behind.'

'You never want to come,' Darryl said in exasperation.

Eleanor shivered involuntarily. He knew Eleanor was enjoying her home comforts here in the pub. Bathing in a clean bathroom; eating without needing to clean the dust off the crockery first. But Darryl hadn't complained about her reluctance to visit the house. It had allowed him the freedom of keeping the speed of the renovation a secret.

Since he'd had the go ahead from Richard, the Chief Fire Officer, that the house was structurally sound and they could move back in, he had arranged for electricians, plumbers, plasterers, kitchen fitters, landscapers and more to come to the house. Richard had been a wealth of information of local tradesmen and was only too happy to help. Darryl arranged everything over the two weeks he was in the hospital. Once he had returned to their room in the pub, a prearranged taxi would take him to the house every morning and bring him back early evening. His injuries had meant he wasn't able to go into work, but he could supervise the work going on at the house. But that was a surprise for later.

'Do you remember when we first went to the shop and Stella was making it quite clear she wanted to know how come you were wearing a ring and I wasn't?' Eleanor's hands turned rigid in his, but he was glad she didn't try to jump up again and run off.

'Well, it gave me an idea.' He took the box from his jeans pocket.

'I'm sorry, Darryl, but I don't think it's a good idea.' Eleanor spoke so fast, the sentence sounded as though it was one word.

'You haven't heard it yet.' He opened the box and pulled out a gold chain.

Eleanor stared at it in silence.

'I would never ask you to remove Nick's ring. I know how much he meant to you, and if you still feel you want to keep it on your finger, then that's fine by me. But I was wondering, what if you wore it on a necklace? A necklace like this, then it would still be close to you.'

Eleanor continued to stare at the chain.

Darryl knew he'd done the wrong thing as soon as he saw her eyes full of tears.

'I was only trying to help,' he mumbled. 'It was a daft idea. I'm sorry.' He quickly closed the box and went to put it back in his pocket, but Eleanor stopped him. Tears rolled down her face and ran round the edges of an enormous smile.

'I thought —' she stammered. 'I thought — it doesn't matter what I thought.'

Darryl's head was hurting with confusion. 'Is this good or not good?' he asked.

'This is good,' she whispered.

Though relieved, Darryl still didn't understand. 'Then why are you crying?'

Eleanor laughed at him.

'You are always protecting me,' she said.

'No, I'm not,' Darryl said defiantly. 'I want to, but, like last night, when I wake up in the middle of the night to find you crying, I feel totally useless. There's nothing I can do to help.'

'But you do help. You're there for me. You hold me till I feel I can breathe again. That's the best thing you can do for me. Nightmares haunt in the middle of the night. That's what nightmares do and nothing you or I do will stop that.' She removed her ring from her finger and threaded the new chain through the centre, fastening it around her neck before letting it hang. Always close to her heart. 'I will get stronger, but you have to trust me. It will take time. Stop trying to protect me, whether it's from nightmares or from nosy neighbours who can't mind their own business. I - I need to apologise to you,' Eleanor added tentatively.

'Apologise? What for?'

'You were right. All my wild theories and suspicions. Me and my pushing nearly got you killed.'

Eleanor looked away and gazed vacantly at the window, not

wanting to face him. Darryl knew how painful the memory was. He had felt it himself. He reached up and turned her head to face him.

'Actually, it nearly got us both killed. But, without you and your wild theories, Carl would still be out there killing, and Stella would still be manipulating him. If you hadn't pushed, the real culprits would never have been caught.'

'Thank you. For understanding,' she clarified. 'But please, just one more thing. No more secrets.'

Darryl wanted to make that promise, but he had one more surprise he had to break to her.

'What about the house?' he asked tentatively.

Eleanor let out a groan and wiped her tear-stained face with the palms of her hands. 'The state of the house is... shall we say, just a little overwhelming? But only an archaeologist with a penchant for old relics wouldn't think so. You don't need to protect me from the house, either.' She leaned back nonchalantly on the bed. 'I'm quite happy to stay here in the pub for as long as it takes for you to get it sorted.'

'I do have another surprise for you,' Darryl said apologetically.

The smile on Eleanor's face dropped. 'I don't think I can cope with any more surprises.'

'I'm pretty certain you're going to like this one. Come on.'

Darryl pulled her by the hand and hobbled down the stairs, out to the taxi he had waiting for his usual morning trip to the house.

Eleanor, dragged along, glanced at herself in the mirror as she passed. The chain hung around her neck with the ring just hidden beneath her blouse. It hung there, feeling like it belonged.

Once sat on the back seat of the taxi, Darryl took hold of Eleanor's hand and insisted she closed her eyes. She was pretty certain she knew where they were going, but, for Darryl's sake, she tried to act excited. Inside the car, she couldn't shake a heavy sense of dread.

The journey seemed longer than usual, the darkness of her eyelids prolonging her suspense. The car slowed and swerved, first to the left, then right and a sharp left again. They had reached Black Spot Bridge. The squeeze of Darryl's hand confirmed it. Would either of them ever be able to pass that point again without remembering what had happened? What *could* have happened?

A few minutes more and she heard the familiar sound of the car driving onto the gravel driveway, and they came to a gentle stop. Eleanor felt a wave of nausea, but she tried not to show it as Darryl helped her out of the car. He led her by the hands across the gravel until she stepped onto soft ground. The small gate clicked shut after them. It wasn't difficult to imagine the grin on Darryl's face as he led her excitedly along the grassy path that led to the back door. He helped her carefully over the threshold and into the house.

'I bet you can't guess where we are,' Darryl said.

'We're at the house,' Eleanor replied, a little more forcefully than she had intended.

'No,' Darryl said quietly. 'We're home. Open your eyes.'

Eleanor opened her eyes and the dark dusty kitchen she remembered was light, bright, and beautiful. They had painted most of the grey stone walls white, leaving a few large stones revealed round the door frames and the windows. The cabinets were white and sleek, reflecting the light from spotlights that gleamed from the ceiling. It was a clean, modern kitchen, but Darryl had still kept its integrity, the history he so loved.

'How have you done all this? There hasn't been time.'

'As soon as Richard gave us the go ahead, everything fell into place. We had already done the hard part, making decisions, ordering the windows, all the preparation. I just called all the tradesmen and, after what had happened to us, they all swarmed to the house, eager to help. It's been chaotic but, as you can see, they've done an amazing job.'

Eleanor heard a loud thud from the hallway and turned to look curiously at Darryl.

'Yeah, I will admit they haven't yet done the entire house, but the kitchen, bathroom, lounge and... and I have to show you this.'

She laughed at Darryl's enthusiasm. He was always full of energy when he was excited about something. She was pulled by the hand out into the hallway, noticing a new fire alarm that had been fixed to the ceiling on her way and no sign of the fire damage. The noise she had heard had come from two men that looked to be fixing the front door.

'I thought the fire ruined the front door.'

'It did,' Darryl said, 'but these guys work up at Minstrelwood and are experts in their field. They have been working on this ever since the fire happened.'

The two men did their best at acknowledging Darryl's compliments, but the door was heavy and not quite on its hinges. They returned quickly to their job before it toppled completely.

'They have built a replica of the original. They've sourced the same beautiful oak and handmade all the ironwork themselves.'

Eleanor examined the door. Every black bolt and hinge were just how she remembered it. All it lacked were the dents and scuffs from hundreds of years of toil. Before she could take in any more, Darryl grabbed her hand again and pulled her through the door and out to the front garden. A gravel footpath that was usually lined with brambles was now bordered with rose bushes. At the furthest end, by the road, he elaborately presented a new post box. It stood proudly, glistening in its shiny black paint by the front gate. 'Shaun no longer has an excuse to come up to the house.'

Eleanor laughed loudly, but Darryl dragged her back towards the house before she could voice any kind of appreciation.

'But there's more to show you inside,' he said.

Eleanor could hardly take it all in while Darryl gabbled excitedly.

'Upstairs, the main bedroom is, of course, finished to perfection, no more sleeping in the dining room, but I've also made sure that one of the other bedrooms is in a decent state for any visitors because I'm not sleeping on that sofa again.'

'That's good,' came a voice from behind them.

Eleanor didn't recognise the voice and turned curiously.

'I was wondering where we were going to sleep tonight,' the girl continued.

Eleanor immediately guessed who the two girls were that entered their front gate. Their faces were identical.

'Alex, Kathy,' Darryl exclaimed. 'You're — you're — It's so good to see you.'

Both girls dropped their bags and ran at their dad, throwing their arms around each other. Eleanor patiently waited until they came apart.

'Girls,' Darryl eventually said. 'This is Eleanor,'

The closest of the girls, her dark hair tied back in a ponytail and dressed like her dad in old jeans and a baggy t-shirt stepped forward. 'Hi, I'm Kathy,' she said as she leaned forward and pecked Eleanor on the cheek. 'It's lovely to meet you.'

The second wore her hair down over her shoulders, and a colourful blouse tied into a knot at her waist over skinny jeans.

She threw her arms around Eleanor and hugged her like a bear. 'I'm Alex and it's so good to meet you at last.'

'Come on inside,' Darryl said, laughing at Eleanor's reaction to the full body hug she received from Alex. He took hold of one of the large rucksacks that had been dumped on the ground, put his arm around Kathy's shoulders and they walked towards the house together.

Alex let go of her grip and said quietly to Eleanor, 'Thanks for making Dad happy again.'

'I hope,' Eleanor said, 'you'll be pleased to know that he makes me happy, too. A little bit crazy sometimes, but mostly happy.'

'Yeah, know that one.' Alex pulled a face while picking up her rucksack and slinging it over her shoulder. She trotted down the path to catch up with her dad and sister.

Eleanor watched as Darryl and his two daughters walked down the path towards the house. She felt for her ring still hanging on the necklace round her neck and held it tight.

'Yeah, a little bit crazy, but mostly happy.'

ENJOYED NEVER OUT OF MIND?

Thanks for reading! If you enjoyed *Never Out of Mind* stay tuned to find out more about the next book in the series, *One Good Turn Deserves Nothing*.

Her failed attempt to save a choking man's life has left her the prime suspect for murder.

When a man at the next table starts choking, Eleanor Garrett is the first to jump in and help. His subsequent death leaves her distraught. Even more so at the discovery it was murder.

The old man's cantankerous disposition has left the police with no shortage of suspects, Eleanor being top of the list.

With mounting evidence, can Eleanor clear her name and find justice?

Books in the Series

- Neither Safe nor Sorry
- Never Out of Mind